# ROBIN HOOD, M.D.

# ROBIN HOOD, M.D.

NEIL SHULMAN, M.D.

authorHOUSE®

*AuthorHouse™ LLC*
*1663 Liberty Drive*
*Bloomington, IN 47403*
*www.authorhouse.com*
*Phone: 1-800-839-8640*

*Published by AuthorHouse  03/24/2014*

*ISBN: 978-1-4969-0001-2 (sc)*
*ISBN: 978-1-4969-0000-5 (e)*

# CONTENTS

# INTRODUCTION

Theodore Bexley Jr. usually had a driver, but on this particular day, in a fit of spontaneity, he decided to drive himself. He, of course, drove a Mercedes Benz. He worked hard and deserved to drive the very best. His suit was more expensive than his first vehicle, a 1976 Camaro. He was dressed for success. He was a captain of industry and he lived the part in every aspect of his life.

He walked to his car with a confident stride. He reached for his "clicker" and pointed it towards the car. He didn't feel the presence of the stranger who had stepped out of the bushes, until it was too late. He suddenly felt something cold and steel pressed into his back and he heard the words, "If you want to live, you will obey my every command. If you don't want to live, tell me now and I will kill you here in the parking lot. I do not care what happens to me at this point. I am happy to die with you if need be." The masked gunman pushed the CEO of Henkins Commerce Insurance Company into the driver's seat of his vehicle. The gunman got into the back of the car.

"Sir, I'm not sure why you're angry at me, but I assure you that we can work this out. You want my credit cards? Cash? What do you want?" Theodore wheezed, starting to reach for his wallet. "Just please don't kill me."

"Start the car," the kidnapper barked. "You have held patients hostage for quite some time; now the tables are turned."

# CHAPTER ONE

"I want you to drive to Maryland Avenue and take a left." Theodore pulled the car out of the parking lot and merged onto the main thoroughfare. "Where are you taking me and what do you want?" Theodore was horrified when the gunman fired a round into the passenger seat. The noise of the gunfire was ear shattering. He screamed, grasping for his roaring ear and ran off the road. He came to a stop in the emergency lane. "Now, Ted," the assailant said in an eerily soft voice, "do I have your full attention?"

"Yes sir," the now tearful CEO whimpered. "Please don't kill me; I don't want to die." In the chaos, Theodore had urinated all over his three thousand dollar suit.

The gunman laughed, "Now Teddy, A big CEO like you shouldn't be pissing in his pants like a frightened 6-year-old. Hell, with all those denial letters you send to patients, I thought you would be a stone cold, heartless son of a bitch who wouldn't be scared of anything. I was apparently mistaken; I guess you have some human qualities after all."

"I--I'm sorry for whatever I denied for you. I--I can make it right," the CEO stammered.

"We *are* going to make something right; you can be assured of that. Keep driving and calm down. Take the next right. At the next light, turn into the parking lot and pull behind the U-Haul truck."

Without risking saying another word, Theodore followed directions and parked behind the truck. "Get out and open the truck door and get in," the kidnapper ordered. Theodore did as he was told. He was sure the truck was where his assailant was really going to let him have it. Theodore Bexley Jr. was not one in the habit of praying...now he was finding himself wishing he'd spent more time 'getting to know the Lord,' as his brother called it. For the first time in his life, Theodore had an earnest one-to-one with his creator. *I'm sorry for cheating the IRS, I'm sorry I've put off giving the mail-room guys the raise I've been promising, I'm sorry I've ignored you, God. I'll do anything you want to make it up to you. I'll even go to church. Just please, please don't let him kill me! I'm too young to die. I need to see my children grow up. Please don't let him kill me!*

Theodore continued to hope against hope for divine intervention as he opened the truck door and was followed by the masked man into the truck. The door was closed and a light was turned on. Theodore was surprised to see that the inside of the truck was converted into an office with carpet, a chair, a desk, and a filing cabinet. "I'm going to interview you. I want you to read a statement I've prepared, and then sign the statement." The kidnapper motioned for him to sit down and then fiddled with something behind a box that was facing Theodore's chair. The gunman's mask stayed on. It unnerved Theodore as much as anything else that he couldn't see who he was dealing with. He'd always hated Halloween.

"After the interview," the masked man announced: "as a condition to being released alive and well, I want you to authorize a bone marrow transplant for one of your patients. You and your insurance company have denied this potentially life-saving procedure for this child. In your denial letter you offered an appeals process. You will authorize the treatment under the auspice of an approved appeal. You will notify the treatment team at St. Jude's hospital to proceed today with the procedure while you are personally preparing the paperwork."

Trying to control the warbling of his voice, the CEO read the statement, "I, Theodore Bexley Jr., am a criminal of the worst kind. I steal your healthcare dollars and profit from your suffering. I am much more dangerous than the common criminal. On a daily basis, I trade the welfare of patients for the wealth of a corporation. As the chief executive officer of this corporation, I personally benefit from the denial of access to healthcare of these patients. My $450,000,000 a year salary is based on the collection of money from our clients and a concerted effort to minimize outflow of payments. At the very least we make every effort to delay payments so that we {float} money and live off the interest. When the stock market is bad, we {float} the money even longer. We answer only to our shareholders. We own Congress because we own the congressmen. We contribute heavily to both parties, and our lobbyists are the best in the business. We give the Congress anything it wants. In turn, they leave us alone. We make it look as though we monitor the quality of healthcare provided, but it is just a facade. We hire physicians and pharmacists to monitor quality. What we really hire them for is to make the doctors prescribe the cheapest generic drugs, or the ones for which we have negotiated a better price with the manufacturer. We never ask the doctors to prescribe the more expensive drugs, even if they are a better choice. We always delay payment of claims by any means possible, moral or amoral. Expensive studies are always prior authorized. We delay the ordering of expensive testing under the umbrella of quality of care.

In summary, I am guilty of crimes against humanity. I am guilty of moral turpitude and the crime of theft by deception. I have the option of a punishment of death, or I will make restitution by righting an ongoing wrong."

"Which do you choose?" asked the masked vigilante.

"Yes, yes, of course, I'll authorize the bone marrow transplant!"

"Well, let's get on with it before you let the kid die. I want you to sign this statement." Theodore did as he was told.

Theodore was handed the folder of the case in question. The patient was a 17 year old black male who had end stage leukemia and had failed on conventional chemotherapy. Henkins Commerce had denied the bone marrow transplant on the basis that it appeared heroic, and the likelihood of success was very low. The best option, according to the insurance company, was to place the 17 year old patient on Hospice. They offered an appeals process as a matter of course. There were multiple letters in the file from the oncologist caring for the young man. The text ranged from an explanation of the medical facts to begging for the patient to be allowed to be saved by the transplant. The doctors had called on multiple occasions.

Theodore read the file and reasoned that the kidnapper must be a family member of the kid. "Sir, I'll be glad to call and fix this mess. I'm sorry this happened."

He actually felt a little sorry for the kid and his family.

The masked gunman threw another folder on the desk and raised his voice. "I want to make it very clear what will happen to you and your family if you go to the police."

"I promise…"

"Shut the hell up," interrupted the attacker. "I want to show you how close I am to your family." Theodore felt like vomiting as he looked at pictures of his three children sleeping in their beds. There were pictures of his parents working in their flower garden. There was a close up photograph of his brother sitting in a golf cart. The most disturbing pictures were taken at his children's elementary school. This nut had close-up pictures of his children playing on the playground and making arts and crafts in the classroom. The final pictures were of Theodore's girlfriend. There were pictures of their apartment in the city. One photograph showed the two of them leaving the residence and engaged in a romantic embrace.

Theodore could no longer sit quietly, "How in God's name did you get all of this information about me? You were in my fucking house taking pictures of my family! My kids, for God's sake! Please don't hurt my kids. Please, do not hurt my kids!" Theodore Bexley had lost all composure. He was screaming and crying. He approached the gunman who slapped him to the floor of the truck.

"Calm down. Nobody will get hurt as long as you do what I say. I am serious about exposing your affair, and hurting or killing your family members if you go to the police. If I have full cooperation, then there will be no need for any violence. If I even think you have contacted the cops, I will unleash a hell on earth on you that you cannot imagine.

"Go and have the seat in your car fixed. If anyone thinks this is a gunshot, tell them your pistol went off in the car. It's unlikely that anyone will notice. Call the hospital and get the bone marrow transplant going. You will also need to send a letter from your office. Your staff will find this odd. Pull rank on them and tell them that you look over these cases on occasion, and that in this case, you decided to allow coverage. Tell the staff it is a good will gesture that will be very important for public relations. Now, get out of here and get to work. I will be monitoring the bone marrow case and it had better go forward today. You will never know how or when I am monitoring you, but as you can see from the folder, I have the capability to invade every aspect of your life. If you change your ways and do the right thing, you will not hear from me again. If you continue to hold America hostage, I will return the favor."

# CHAPTER TWO

"Dr. Jameson, I have the CEO of Henkins Commerce Insurance Company on the telephone and he wants to talk directly to the doctor in charge of Timothy Sims," the surprised ward clerk said. Dr. Jameson was puzzled but reached for the phone anyway.

"I am authorizing the bone marrow transplant on Timothy Sims," said the voice on the other end of the line.

"Who is this?" retorted the exhausted doctor. He had had a long day, and doubted he'd heard correctly. Wishful thinking was all it was.... or a prank call. He looked at the caller ID display –the call was indeed coming from Henkins Commerce. "The clerk said you're the CEO of Mr. Sim's insurance company. Why are you calling me yourself?"

"I've reviewed the case and it seems that our client would benefit from a transplant. I have the fax number on the ward and for your office, and I'll send a written notice of our decision and an authorization code number." Dr. Jameson was stunned. He couldn't think of a word to say in response. He'd never in all his years of practice seen an insurance company display such a sudden turnaround. The voice came through the receiver again. "Are you there, Doctor?"

Dr. Jameson struggled to find his voice again: "Yes. I'm here. I—I just, I'm a little surprised. I—I'll get the ball rolling on this end right away." The doctor started to come fully to his senses again as he realized what a mess the whole situation had become. "I've sent the patient home on hospice. I thought, because you denied the transplant, he was certain to die. I told the family he was going to die. They're making funeral arrangements as we speak." The doctor felt a deep surge of anger well up inside. He struggled to maintain a professional distance as he pressed the chief executive officer. "Would you mind telling me why you didn't approve this earlier? It was obvious that this procedure needed to be done." The CEO held his tongue, and the doctor continued.

"This kid was referred to me by his family doctor two years ago. He was one hell of a football player. As only a sophomore, he was being scouted by fifteen division one schools. He was rated by some scouts as the number one running back in the country. He would have had two more years to play if he had not gotten ill."

"When he began bruising excessively at every game, his doctor discovered an elevated white count and sent him to me. I did a bone marrow biopsy and diagnosed acute myelocytic leukemia. We began chemotherapy right away, but had little success. I did everything in my power to get him into remission, but he has a resistant case of leukemia which is untreatable. We expressly indicated to your company that the only remaining possibility was a bone marrow transplant."

Theodore Bexley Jr. dared not interrupt Dr. Jameson's rant. The doctor continued. "His brother, Thad, was a perfect match. We told the family that we had a treatment that could be life saving, and they agreed to proceed. This is where your company gave us a red light. You said that you would review the case and that it may take up to two months. I wrote you letters. The family wrote you letters. The head of staff at the hospital wrote you letters. And your company had the nerve to deny the transplant. What, if you don't mind my frankness, what in the hell were you thinking to deny this transplant for so long?"

"Doctor, I know you are upset, but I wish to rectify the situation."

"It may be too late! This kid's father is livid that his son couldn't have the transplant. I thought he was going to slit my throat when I told him. He blamed me for not giving his child the transplant."

Theodore gulped, "I am sorry our company waited so long to make our decision. I hope it's not too late for our client."

"If this transplant doesn't work out because we waited too long, Mr. Bexley, I do hope that you lose as much sleep over this as I have. For Christ's sake, I don't know how you insurance people live with yourselves!" The doctor slammed down the phone and turned to the nurse who was checking charts at the desk beside him. "I need you to get the Sims family on the phone immediately."

The Sims were a very tight-knit family. They lived in a modest home and the parents both worked very hard to make "ends meet."

The father, John, worked as a brick layer. He made a decent salary, but did not have benefits. Health insurance was not offered by his employer. He worked from daybreak to darkness and he hated his manual labor job. He worked for his kids. He told his kids on a weekly basis to, "study hard and stay in school, so you can get a desk job. You can make $500 per week and work inside. I have to bust my ass every day and I take home less than half of that in a week." He loved his children very much. He didn't understand why the doctors could not help his son.

Saurina worked as a custodian at the local hospital. She personally knew the doctors who cared for her son, Tim. The salary was not great, but she had good health insurance, or so she had thought. The insurance company had no problem collecting the premium. It was payroll deducted. She paid one third of her $250 per week paycheck towards health insurance. The hospital paid the other portion of the premium. She had actually felt safe when she looked at the insurance card and saw her family's name listed on it. She learned this was all one big lie when Dr. Jameson delivered the ominous news to the family.

"The insurance company apparently is not going to pay for the transplant," the doctor had said, heaving a great sigh of resignation. "I'm sorry I don't have anything else to offer Timothy. I'm releasing him today to hospice care." Saurina felt she'd had the wind knocked out of her when she learned that the insurance which she worked so hard for was worth nothing, and that none of her personal connections at the hospital could change anything. It was funny; the strange little things one noticed when a death sentence was delivered... the mismatched paneling in the ceiling, the sign above every door that read "Have a nice day!" Everyone's skin seemed illuminated with a slightly blue tinge under the fluorescent lighting. She noticed that the doctor's eyes were bloodshot and swollen, as if he had either been up all night grappling with the prognosis or had been crying...or both. The doctor had lingered long enough to answer any questions and then humbly excused himself, trudging away from the grieving family as if he had lead in his pockets. None in the family doubted the sincerity of the poor doctor's efforts.

Saurina had sent the others home when she came to, and asked for the preacher and family to gather at the house. She knew she was going to need a lot of support to bring her son home to die. In a daze, she began to pack up all of the belongings that had found their way into his hospital room; his football jersey, his trophies and medals, the mountain of photos, flowers, and get-well cards sent by friends and team-mates. As she made for the bathroom to collect her son's toiletries, bathrobe in hand, she froze mid -stride and turned to look back at him. Her big strong boy looked so frail. Wasn't it just yesterday he had bounded over to her after a game and lifted her right off her feet as he spun her around in excitement? Now he could barely lift his head off the pillow to give her a weak smile when he noticed her gazing at him. He was her first born child, and though each of her children were equally loved, he was extra special to her. Of their three kids, he was the one who had always had an uncanny ability to read her thoughts and actions. Whenever she was having a bad day he was the first to pick up on it.

He had always been alert and active, even as an infant. Everyone got a kick out of the way he always held his arms out in front of him, as if ready to catch a ball. All of the great aunts chuckled over how cute it was, but her father had predicted, "I do believe young Timothy's a ball player." He had leaned down and gently whispered in the cooing baby's ear: "You make your mama proud, okay there, little running back?" Saurina's father had passed away the year before Timothy entered high school, but Tim kept his grandpa's picture in his wallet, and taped inside the door of his locker. How quickly 17 years had passed…She remembered so vividly the night they brought him home from the hospital as a newborn, how everyone had gathered in the living room to admire her perfect new baby and welcome him to the world. Now they were gathering to say goodbye forever to the young man who would always be her baby. 'Got to be strong, Saurina!' she told herself, 'Got to be strong for your little Tim.' She gazed down at him, blurring before her eyes, and wondered how long she'd been sobbing. She made several attempts to speak before croaking: "Tim, baby, I'm sorry. I'm so sorry. God, I'm sorry. I worked hard for that insurance. My baby, please forgive me."

"Mom it's okay, it's not your fault. I want to go home. It's over." He took his mom's hand and tried to comfort her. 'Just like my boy,' Saurina thought bleakly to herself, 'always trying to make me feel better when he's hurting. How are we going to live without him?'

The family's church was New Life Gospel and Holiness Tabernacle. The Apostle Joseph Henderson was the Pastor. As Tim's condition had worsened, he had tried to comfort the family by reminding them with great exuberance, "God has a plan for us all. We must turn this situation over to Him and accept that we are powerless. We must rest in Jesus and know that God has His hand on every one of us."

Pastor Henderson was the first to arrive at the Sims house to welcome Tim home one final time. He tried to console Timothy's father, but Mr. Sims was too stressed to be comforted by anything the preacher could say. Mr. Sims kept shaking his head and repeating, "it ain't right, it ain't right what they've done to my boy. It just can't be. You sure they ain't made a mistake?"

Normally a calm man under any circumstance, the minister had finally lost his composure when he learned that it was a financial decision made by the insurance company that was to cost this young man his life. He began to cry and scream at God in front of the family and the gathered friends. "If he had money, he would get the transplant! If he had another color of skin, he would get the transplant! If he lived in another country that had free healthcare, he would get the transplant! If he lived in another community, he would get the transplant!" he ranted. "God, we just don't understand! You're a good God! You're a just God! Why are you doing this? Why? Tell me or strike me down now! Why?!! Now I'm asking you, if it be your will, Lord God, spare this boy. Save him! If it's your will, Heavenly Father, I'm asking for a miracle."

Friends and family heard the news and began to prepare for the homecoming of Timothy Sims. The tradition of cooking for any neighbor with an illness in the family was longstanding. The worse the tragedy, the larger the quantities of food. The Sims home was canvassed with food; pot roasts, rice dishes, fried chicken, peach cobblers, and all kinds of casseroles and pies. No one was going to be hungry for a while.

As Timothy was wheeled into the house by his mother, everyone scrambled to be the first to greet him at the door. He was patted, hugged, squeezed, and pinched as he was wheeled into the living room. With all the commotion going on, at first no one noticed the phone ringing.

Finally, Thad heard it and called, "Hey Mom, get the phone!"

It was hard to pull away from the group, but finally she broke from the others to pick up, annoyed at the persistence of the caller, muttering to herself, "What could be so important?" She initially spoke softly, so she wouldn't interrupt the gathering. Suddenly, everyone turned to look at her as she loudly rebutted; "Dr. Jameson, what is this? I just got him home. Why do I need to bring him back to the hospital? I don't want to hear another thing about that goddamned insurance company!"

John shouted from the living room: "Hang up that phone! Leave my family alone!" Mrs. Sims held the telephone away from her ear after hearing Dr. Jameson deliver the unlikely news, and then fell to the floor. The phone struck the ground as John and the family ran to her.

Preacher Henderson picked up the phone. "Now, what's this?"

"The insurance company has called and they're going to pay for the bone marrow transplant." Dr. Jameson reiterated quickly to be sure he'd get it out before being hung up on. "I am sending an ambulance to pick up Timothy. I know this is hard to believe. I had the same response. I am sending a letter with the ambulance personnel. It has a number on it for verification purposes. I have just received the fax from the CEO of the insurance company."

Preacher Henderson was animated at times during his sermon, but this beat all anyone had ever seen. His vertical leap could have rivaled any NBA player as he jumped and let out a scream that was ear shattering: "Hallelujah! Thank you, Lord! Amen! Jesus said, [ask and you shall receive]. I asked, no, I begged Jesus today, and He answered our prayers!" He was sobbing as he embraced Tim. "God has a miracle in store for you today, Timothy Sims!" Bedlam erupted in the house. Everyone was dancing and crying. The preacher shouted, "Oh God, we were in a valley, and now you pulled us to the top of the mountain! We were walking through the valley of the shadow of death, and you gave us life!"

Dr. Jameson had dispatched an ambulance to the residence of Timothy Sims. The emergency medical technicians heard the ruckus in the house from outside. The doorbell and the usual light knock on the door rendered no response. A much harder rap on the door and front window was required in order to get the attention of the celebrating family. When the family saw the ambulance, the celebration increased. Timothy's mother had awakened and the reality of the miracle was beginning to set in. When she saw her son being placed into the ambulance, and she reviewed the document from the insurance company, she turned to her husband in wonder: "this is really going to happen. I can't believe it. Our baby's getting his transplant." John Sims was too choked up to respond.

# CHAPTER THREE

———•◦≈◦•———

Jonathan Willingham was a graduate of the Harvard MBA program. He was highly recruited and had landed a job at a large health insurance company. Within ten years, he had worked himself up through middle level management, and eventually was inaugurated as the chief executive officer of the company. The $349,000,000 per year salary was well earned. He worked extremely hard and carried a heavy load of responsibility. The shareholders and the board of directors wanted continued financial success. They didn't care about anything else.

He worked late that day. The board meeting ended at 8 pm, and, as was usually the case, the meeting after the meeting ensued. The board of directors had unanimously given the CEO of Fulton Christian Hall Insurance Company its vote of confidence, and he was summarily congratulated. It was 9:15 pm before he made it to his car.

He was very tired, and therefore, totally oblivious to his surroundings as he got off the elevator at his private office parking garage. He opened the driver's side door and got behind the wheel, never noticing the intruder in the back seat. No sooner was his key in the ignition, that he began struggling to breath. He soon lost consciousness.

Jonathan slowly regained consciousness. He didn't know how long it was that he drifted between waking and sleeping. It was a sharp pain in his right hand which finally jarred him into a fully awake state. He tried to move away from the pain, but soon realized that he was restrained. A figure was slowly moving towards him. Though it was dark, Jonathan could just make out that the person appeared to be wearing a mask. He was carrying something in his right hand.

"Mr. Willingham, do you have health insurance?" asked the dim figure approaching him.

"What in the hell is going on here? Who are you? Where am I? What are you doing to me?"

The masked man took a red marker and wrote the words SELF PAY on the CEO's bare chest.

"I guess that means you do not have health insurance. Don't feel badly; having insurance isn't all it's cracked up to be. You can pay those bastards premiums for years, and then you get sick," the madman began to inject something into the intravenous needle in Jonathan's right arm, "and all of the sudden, you're paying for everything yourself. The term that hospitals use is self pay."

Everything went black again. A wave of nausea swept over the CEO and he began to vomit. Jonathan began to shake uncontrollably and then he passed out.

He awoke feeling as if he'd been run over by a truck. It was worse than the worst hang-over he'd ever experienced in his college drinking days. However, he could have handled feeling like just plain shit, if it were not compounded by the feeling of terror and impending doom as he began to realize that he had been kidnapped. This fucking psychopath who was restraining him had apparently injected him with some type of medication. He heard the beeping of a medical monitor. He turned his head slowly, so as not to anger this animal, and noted a heartbeat tracing on a monitor. He had never been in a hospital before. He only recognized it from the medical dramas he sometimes skimmed past on late night TV. He did not see the kidnapper in the room. He hoped that whoever this was, he was through with his experiment. He heard a door open behind him and footsteps approaching, and then silence. He turned around and looked over his left shoulder. Goddamned psycho was playing tricks on him, making him think he was going crazy.

"How do you feel?" said the voice of the masked man, who leaned in close and spoke suddenly in the CEO's other ear. The CEO winced from where the I.V. needle pulled in his hand.

Not knowing how else to answer this guy and not wanting to irritate the sick bastard, he answered truthfully, "To tell you the truth, I feel pretty rough. I have a horrible headache and I think I might vomit." The masked man didn't respond. Made nervous by the lack of response, the CEO pleaded, "Please don't hurt me."

The kidnapper gave an irreverent snort, and then left the room. He returned about half an hour later with a large and a small syringe. He was wearing surgical attire. He had on a surgical mask, hat, and scrubs. Jonathan was wide awake now, and more terrified than ever. "Do you know what it feels like do be in a diabetic coma?" the kidnapper demanded of the non- consenting patient.

"No, sir," the executive whispered hoarsely.

"You've been in and out of one for several hours, so you actually do. You just were not aware of it. Now that you know how it feels to make wild swings between very high and very low blood sugar levels, I wanted to ask you if you want to get back on the ride again." The captor held up the syringes to the patient. "The big one is glucose, or sugar. The small one is insulin. I have placed you in insulin shock, and then I rescued you with glucose." Each syringe was dangled immediately in front of the captive's nose for effect.

Jonathan Willingham screamed, "Please, sir, don't do that again to me. You could kill me doing that shit to my body. My body won't take this kind of abuse."

The captor walked away and began to slowly pace around the bed. He began, "Do you think that any human being should be subjected to this kind of treatment?"

The captive whined, "Hell no, they shouldn't!"

"Nobody, you say?" the captor demanded, his raised voice trembling slightly.

"N-no. No, sir," the CEO squeaked, hoping he hadn't now offended the kidnapper.

"Okay, then," the captor barked, "Why in the hell do you treat your clients like this? This is exactly what your doing to Debra Justin. What happened to you today is only a glimpse into her hellish life."

The CEO dared not argue with this psychopath, for fear of another shot of insulin.

The kidnapper continued, "Debra has had the misfortune of having diabetes since she was a small child. She was excited to have a new job because she would have a pay increase. She never thought the change in insurance coverage would nearly cost her life. She read the words, "pre-existing condition," but did not understand the implications. When she took her prescription for long acting insulin to the pharmacy, she was told she didn't have coverage for her diabetes medications and supplies. The prescriptions would cost her nearly what her salary was after taxes. She learned the same day that her doctor's visits would not be paid for if the reason for the visit was diabetes. She was devastated and terrified." The attacker turned his back to his prey and took a deep breath. The silence was more frightening than the verbal assault.

The kidnapper finally continued, "A lack of medical care and a change to cheaper and less effective insulin has nearly cost the young lady her life. She has been in the intensive care unit six times this year for serious diabetic complications. She has experienced much worse than you have today. The whole time that she has been sick," the captor's voice rose with a tremor, "she has continued to pay premiums to your company because she needs insurance. Your company has not paid one penny of her $400,000 medical bills, so to stop the harassment of the collection agency for the hospital, she is going to have to file bankruptcy. This defies her morals, but she has no choice in the matter."

"Sorry," wheezed the CEO, his throat knotting as he wondered what his captor was going to do next to him to get even.

"Are you sorry you're about to die, or are you sorry for what you've done?"

"Sorry for what I've done," the executive pleaded in what he hoped was a convincing tone of voice.

"We must pay for our sins. You have raped and pillaged your clientele. These are innocent people who have put their physical well being in your hands, only to learn of your real intentions when they become ill," the captor preached.

"If you want to live, you will read a statement which I have prepared. I will give you an opportunity to overturn a heinous decision that your greedy company has made.

In addition, you are going to personally purchase a one year supply of insulin for Debra Justin and have a courier deliver it to her house. You will lift the pre-existing condition from her claim denials, and you will pay every past and present claim. Finally, you will donate $100,000 to the American Diabetes Association."

The restraints and the intravenous catheter were removed and the command given to: "clean up and get ready to read the prepared statement."

"I, Jonathan Willingham, am a criminal of the worst kind....

In summary, I am guilty of crimes against humanity. I am guilty of moral turpitude and theft by deception." He gulped as he read the end of the statement, "I have the option of a punishment of death, or I will make restitution by righting an ongoing wrong."

"Which do you choose?" asked the captor.

"I will, of course, do as you asked for the diabetic patient."

"If you take care of business, you will never hear from me again. However, I will cause great harm to you and your family if you call the police, or if you notify anyone of our encounter. Do you think I'm joking with you?"

"No sir," the captive replied obediently.

The kidnapper showed the CEO a pictorial display of his family. Many of the pictures were very candid.

"Leave us alone! Please! I'll do anything you want! Just leave us alone!" the CEO screamed.

"Keep your damn mouth shut and I will. Put on this blindfold and I'll take you back to your car."

The CEO pulled the blindfold over his eyes and was led out to a running vehicle where he was none too gently pushed into the back seat. They drove in silence for some time before the kidnapper spoke. "I'm sorry things have gotten so bad that I had to resort to violence, but I see no alternative."

Taken aback at the shift in tone, the CEO stammered, "That's—it's fine."

"No, really, I don't want to be the bad guy here, but somebody's got to. We just need to make sure people get the proper care, don't you agree?"

"Yes," the CEO agreed.

They small talked the rest of the drive, about everything from sports to fine dining. It was terribly unnerving to Jonathan. To say that he was extremely relieved when they reached his car would be an understatement of the grandest proportion.

"Are you okay to drive?" the kidnapper asked as he pulled off Jonathan's blindfold.

"Yes, I'm-I'm fine."

The CEO was released and the masked kidnapper drove away. Jonathan squinted at the car as it pulled away to see if he could get a tag number, but then recalled the pictures of his family and turned back to opening his own car door. He sat in his car for a few minutes, trembling all over. He let out a sob of relief that he was still alive and in one piece. He turned on the heat full blast but it seemed he would never shake the chills which now racked his body.

The knock on the door startled Debra Justin. She peeked out the window and did not recognize the stranger. She slowly opened the door a crack, leaving the latch at the top of the door fastened. The stranger claimed to be a courier bringing her insulin supplies. She couldn't decide whether to open the door or not. She decided against her better judgment to listen to the stranger. Without any further explanation, he handed her a large container filled with long acting insulin and diabetic supplies. Wordlessly, he retreated to an unmarked black vehicle idling on the street in front of her house, leaving her glued to her porch and staring in disbelief at her enormous supply of her medicine.

# CHAPTER FOUR

—•◦⟨≋⟩◦•—

"Shit! How many times do I have to show you guys how to hand me a surgical instrument?" Dr. Susan Harrison had no tolerance for incompetence. She was tougher on the operating room staff than any of the male surgeons. She made it very clear that she was in control. Unmarried and ferociously independent, she made it clear to all those around her that she was a neurosurgeon because she busted her ass, not because anyone gave her a break. She looked like an angel and cursed like a sailor.

Shortly after finishing her case and discussing the results with the family, her pager went off. She went to the surgical lounge to use the telephone. "What the hell do you mean the insurance company will not pay for the MRI? You tell those sons of bitches that the patient has symptoms of an aneurysm. The only way I can tell if she has the blood vessel defect is to do a magnetic resonance imaging and angiography. She's having terrible, unrelenting headaches. She had a normal CT scan of the head, but that is not sufficient to show if she has an aneurysm of the brain!" She suddenly noticed some disapproving glares coming from a few of the stuffy elderly doctors at a table in the corner of the lounge. She didn't care that she'd spoken loudly enough for other people in the surrounding area and hallway to hear her. She was mad, damn it! She slammed down the phone and glanced at the clock---1:25 pm. She had clinic at 1:30.

She rushed to grab a sandwich on the way to clinic. She ran eight miles at 5 am every day as part of her marathon training. She felt invigorated after the run, but her legs were beginning to ache as the day went on and it made her "hungry as hell" by noon. This was her first marathon, and according to her it would "be her last one too."

Clinic went as usual. Most of the patients were at the visit to plan surgery, or they were postoperative checks. Dr. Harrison had a view panel to look at x-rays in every room. She also had a computer in every room in order to view x-rays available on disk or through the hospital computer system.

The clinic was staffed by both neurologists and neurosurgeons. The patient Dr. Harrison had been in a fit over on the phone earlier that day had been referred to the neurological services by the infirmary to rule out a cerebral aneurysm. The front office staff had made an appointment with Dr. Harrison, a brain surgeon, because the referral mentioned the possibility of an aneurysm. The patient had been seen once before. Dr. Harrison had reviewed the CT scan on the view board with the patient during the last visit. She agreed with the radiologist that the study was normal. However, she had practiced long enough to know from experience that an aneurysm didn't always appear on a CT scan.

Dr. Harrison hated having to meet with patients when her hands were tied. She pulled the chart from the door and entered the room. Natasha had asked her mother to come to the appointment with her. After introductions, Dr. Harrison began, "Natasha, the insurance company is refusing to pay for your MRI. They say that you don't have enough symptoms to warrant the study."

Natasha Kapinski was a graduate student at the local university. She was majoring in international studies. She used the campus infirmary for minor health problems. At the recommendation of the university, she had purchased health insurance. She was told that; "in the event that you have a health problem that the infirmary doctor's cannot treat, you will need health insurance."

"Dr. Harrison, I don't understand! I have headaches every day, and they're getting worse. Why won't they pay for the test?" the patient pleaded.

"What's an aneurysm?" asked Natasha's now concerned mother. "Natasha said you're concerned that she may have one."

The doctor explained; "An aneurysm is a blood vessel in your brain that balloons out. It can cause headaches. In the worst case scenario, the blood vessel can rupture and bleed. This can cause a stroke or even death."

The conversation stood in pause. Natasha and her mother stared at each other for a full minute. A tear rolled down Natasha's cheek, and her mother rose from her chair to comfort her. She stroked her daughter's hair and wiped her tears from her face. "It'll be okay, baby." Mrs. Kapinski cooed, trying to shake aside her own fears.

Dr. Harrison explained: "A CT scan will not show an aneurysm, unless it has already ruptured and is bleeding. The study we need is an MRI and MRA. I am trying to get the study pre-certified."

"What do you have to do so we can get the test done?" Joan Kapinski wondered wearily.

"I have to call the reviewer at the insurance company. This is a physician who is reviewing your case to determine whether you can have an MRI," the doctor explained.

"How can doctors who have never seen me make a decision about what kind of test I can have?" Natasha protested. "This is ridiculous! What if I have something wrong with me and they wait too late to do the MRI?" By this time she was shrill with panic.

Both the patient and her mother were surprised at the anger that suddenly emanated from the doctor. "I am sick and damn tired of the insurance companies telling me how to practice medicine! I apologize for my language, but I'm telling you the truth about medical care today. All the insurance companies give a shit about is making and saving money. They only require pre-certification of expensive tests and medications. I have never heard of an insurance company calling a doctor and asking for them to prescribe a more expensive drug, or to order a more expensive test. They always want the cheaper drugs and less expensive tests. The alpha and omega of the insurance industry is to make money."

Natasha tearfully pondered: "Will they ever pay for the test?"

"Hopefully, they will allow you to have the study. But they're legally entitled to review and pre-certify expensive studies. Then they can delay payment in the name of quality assurance. One of the company's physicians will review the case. I'll call the reviewer and convince him to allow the study to be done. By the time a case is approved, they'll have made interest on the money the clients have paid as premiums. Do the math. If they have 600 million dollars in an interest bearing account collecting five percent annual interest, three weeks equals a bundle of money." The doctor reached in her pocket and pulled out her calculator. "In fact, if we use this as an example, they make over 1.5 million in interest if they hold onto this money for the extra time."

"That is bull shit!" the young patient yelled. "How can they be allowed to do this? How could doctors let the insurance companies take control of the whole medical system?"

Embarrassed for the entirety of modern medicine, Dr. Harrison simply conceded the truth of Natasha's summation in silence. She finally responded, "We have the nuts running the asylum. Things are just absolutely out of hand. Those who pay the bills make the decisions."

Natasha retorted, "I just want to know what's wrong with me and have it fixed. I can't study while taking these pain medications."

The doctor refocused, "I'll get your MRI pre-certified somehow. Let me know if your symptoms worsen and I will meet you in the emergency room. Unlike many radiology studies, an MRI is difficult to get done as an emergency. The staff is available only at certain hours and the radiologists only read the studies on certain days. I can do my best to get it done, or we will do another study which will require you to be admitted to the hospital. This is a dye study called an arteriogram. Let me know if the pain increases."

The visit ended and Dr. Harrison barked to her nurse who jumped out of her chair. "Get the reviewer on the phone!"

"This is Doctor Jones," replied the elderly voice on the other end of the phone.

"What is your specialty, doctor?"

"I'm a retired urologist. I work part time for the insurance company."

Dr. Harrison withheld her scorn and spoke very politely to the reviewer. Her grandmother had always told her that you can catch more flies with honey than shit. She agreed. This was the time to get this study done, not to try to change the system. "Dr. Jones, have you had a chance to review the medical records we faxed to you?"

"Why, yes I have," replied the grandfatherly figure. "I see that this student has headaches and her CT scan was normal. Doctor, I just do not see why we have to go any further on her case. I don't think she needs an MRI. From your exam notes it appears that she doesn't have any neurological deficits, unless there's something I don't see here."

Dr. Harrison had to close her eyes and say a quick version of the serenity prayer in order to prevent an emotional explosion. She wanted to verbally execute this old imbecile. He was probably basing his decision on medical knowledge from 30 to 40 years before the technology of MRI was developed. Likely, his last neurological exam was in medical school. She gritted her teeth in order to stay cool and act friendly.

"Are you still there, Dr. Harrison?" the elder doctor called.

"Yes, I am sorry. I was reviewing the medical record," she lied. "The exam is benign, but the history is worrisome for an aneurysm. She is having worsening headaches, and awakes at night with headaches. She is adopted, so I don't know her family history."

The reviewer rebutted: "If she had a bleeding aneurysm, the CT scan would have shown hemorrhage."

"The scan would have shown a large bleed. Sometimes, it'll show a small one. But a CT scan will never show an aneurysm that's about to rupture," Dr. Harrison groaned.

"I'll have to run this past my supervisor. Appears to me this girl is having simple migraine headaches. Let's try conservative measures first. Let her see a neurologist and see what he thinks. If, in say, two or three weeks she is not better, then I can authorize the study. If my supervisor thinks we can do it now, I'll call you back."

Dr. Harrison was fuming: "I want to go on record to say if, while waiting on your approval, this girl has a bleed, I am going to hold you responsible!"

The reviewer did as he was instructed in training and offered, "Doctor, if at any time she has an emergency, have her go to the emergency room. I'm sorry, but we use certain criteria to approve MRI studies, and this patient does not meet the criteria."

"What in the hell do you think they're going to do with the patient in the emergency room?" Dr. Harrison inquired. "I'm the one they call with a patient who has a cerebral hemorrhage!"

Dr. Jones had not been briefed on how to answer this question. "I—I'm sorry you're upset. I'll ask the supervising reviewer if there's anything I can do."

With concerted effort, Dr. Harrison set the receiver down gently on the telephone base. She checked to see if she had any other patients.

The staff members were silent, awaiting an explosion. She said calmly, "The blood is on the insurance company's hands if something happens to this kid. I am not going to cuss. I am not going to break anything. I've had enough of this garbage. I'm going home to take a hot shower and get ready for dinner. I have a date." The tension, palpable initially, began to subside. Her nurse winked at her as she left the office.

She thought of the case as she stood under the hot water. She lathered and scrubbed herself three times in an attempt to wash this shitty day off her body. She had done all she could and knew nothing else to do but wait. She implored her shoulders to relax under the hot water. She found that there were a few things that she was not in control of. How her body handled stress was one of them. She was not on call so she planned to have a couple of glasses of wine with dinner. Just the thought of the wine caused the tension to release from her neck. She shrugged her shoulders and moved her neck from side to side. She wondered if people with normal jobs dealt with this level of tension. Why did she choose this life? She would have made a good housewife. She could keep a man coming home.

She had been engaged once to a very nice man. His name was William. He was a very attractive man with a good head on his shoulders. The only problem was that he was old fashioned. He wanted a modern woman who had a 1950's housewife values. She wanted to be a brain surgeon. After a long discussion with him about her role in the home, and who was going to raise the two children they were planning on having, she decided to forgo the marriage for her career. Nothing was going to get in the way of her career. On days like today, she wondered why she had sacrificed a normal life for this shit.

At 31, her biological clock was beginning to tick. Away from the glory of her private neurosurgical practice, she felt alone. She hated to admit such a weakness, but as a scientist, she realized that humans are social creatures who yearn for true companionship. William was long gone, so she was trying to find a suitable substitute for him. Her friends and family had all told her she was too picky, but how in the hell could you be too choosy, when it comes to finding a soul-mate?

She noticed her nude profile in the mirror. She turned to the right and admired the increased tone in her abdomen and thighs. She was seeing the results of the marathon training. She had a tremendous body before she began the training. She wore loose clothing and a lab jacket so men wouldn't notice her figure. At work, she wanted to be noticed for her work, not her femininity. Tonight, she wanted George to notice her hot body. She wanted to be a girl tonight, not a doctor.

She stood at the closet, now clad in her finest undergarments, looking at her limited dress selection. She stood in front of the mirror and held several options up to her chest, throwing each of them to the bed in disgust. "Too dressy, too loud, too 'librarian,' she muttered, assessing each choice. "I wish I knew more about this girly dress-up crap," she said to herself. Her expertise came in more when the dress came off! She had always thought more like a man than a woman. She settled on her black low-cut cocktail dress, recalling how her mother had worried about her being a tomboy. "But what kind of a tomboy would wear a dress like this?" she giggled, posing in the mirror as if she were a top model.

This was the six month anniversary of their first date. They had met at the hospital. He had made a sheepish pass at her in the doctor's lounge, and she, to his surprise, accepted the offer for a dinner date. She liked the fact that he didn't come on too strong. He was a family practice doctor and a widower who had lost his wife to cancer. He had no children which was optimal. She didn't want any baggage.

The doorbell shocked her back to reality. She collected her purse and keys, and made her way towards the front door of her modest apartment. She tried not to hurry but did anyway.

She opened the door slowly, as if revealing a concealed gift. She awaited his response.

"You look, I mean, I have never seen you this dressed up," George verbally stumbled.

He felt his heart falter as she turned her head to the side assimilating a response. He was sure he'd blown it and offended her. He'd seen her reduce other male doctors to a pulp for less. She shrugged it off with a grin. "How do I look, mister?"

"You look absolutely... beautiful," he quickly recovered.

She began to laugh loudly, and George was relieved at the release of tension. He was still in awe of her newly displayed beauty as they walked to his car. She lifted his head upwards to meet her eyes, as he conversed with her barely covered breasts. "I love your dress. You look great!"

"Do you think you're going to make it through dinner?" the scantly clad doctor toyed with him.

"I don't think there'll be any movie tonight!" he grinned.

"Maybe we can make our own little movie," Dr. Harrison insinuated. She reached over and touched George's leg.

George almost hit a parked car as the image he had conjured in his mind met with the tactile stimulation of Susan's warm hand. He wondered what had gotten into her. Whatever it was, he approved.

Susan had changed the conversation so at least she could get a pre-intercourse meal in tonight. She told George the story of the insurance company's refusal to allow an MRI on her patient. She wasn't going to bring it up and ruin her evening, but it had begun to gnaw at her brain again. The sexual tension quickly subsided at the change of topic.

"I deal with that bullshit all the time," George began. He turned into the restaurant parking lot as he continued. "Is seafood okay? I know you're not eating red meat during training."

"That's fine. I'm really hungry," she replied wearily. She ate like a starving teenager on the days she trained. She felt a little weak and hoped the food would remedy the problem.

"When we order expensive x-rays, or non-generic medications, we always get a hassle from the insurance companies," Dr. George Stanley sighed. "Why don't we forget about all of that nonsense tonight, and have some fun?"

"I want something to drink. And let's look at the appetizer list right away," Dr. Harrison commanded, as they walked from the parking lot to the lobby of the restaurant. She had fallen out her sensual mood, and was pissed off again as she thought of Natasha. She wondered if her patient was still hurting.

George noted the scowl on her face starting to lift with each sip of wine. She was laughing again within 20 minutes. The appetizers seemed to help her feelings also. She ordered enough food to feed a hungry village in sub-Saharan Africa, and then she proceeded to eat 95% of it. She forgot about her terrible day and enjoyed the dinner. The conversation was absolutely non-medical. They spoke of sports, movies, politics, and nothing more.

"I have to go to the little girls' room," she smiled, standing and waltzing away from the table. She had long since forgotten her stressful day as she walked into the restroom.

The tile in the bathroom cost more than the lumber required to construct the average home. The tile was carved marble. She was surprised that there wasn't a restroom attendant in this 'swanky' joint. "Maybe they had to use the bathroom," she chuckled under her breath. Susan noticed that she was all alone in the restroom, and she was glad for that. She sat on the toilet and began to urinate, when she heard the footsteps of another patron. She really had to fart (wine had that affect on her), but wanted to wait until the other lady had made her way into her own stall. She planned to await the sounds that usually emanated from sitting on a toilet, before beginning her own symphony of gaseous sounds. Instead of proceeding to another stall, the other patron came to a stand still in front of Susan's stall door. Something hit the floor, and to the surprise of Dr. Harrison, was pushed under the bathroom stall door.

# CHAPTER FIVE

DR. SUSAN HARRISON was typed on the outside of the envelope. The lady outside of her door had walked away as she looked at the envelope in disbelief. "How the hell did someone know I was in here?" she muttered to herself. She noted that she was now alone and loudly relieved herself, as she opened the envelope.

IF YOU WANT YOUR PATIENT TO LIVE,
CONTACT ME. I CAN HELP.

ROBIN HOOD M.D. @ SPELLBOUND.NET

Dr. Harrison sat on the toilet another five minutes re-reading the note. She said aloud: "How in God's name could someone know about my patient?" as she adjusted her dress and slowly opened the door. No one was in the restroom. She was terrified as she hurriedly washed her hands and made her way back to the table.

George sat patiently. Susan had been in the restroom for nearly 15 minutes. The waiter had checked 3 times to see if the couple wanted coffee or dessert. George stood to stretch his legs and noticed Susan walking at breakneck speed towards the table. "What's wrong?" George asked.

Dr. Susan Harrison was obviously shaken. As she approached, George noticed a look on her face that he had never seen. He had certainly seen her angry before but this look was different.

"I want to get the hell out of here!" Susan snapped.

The check was paid, and the couple walked silently to the car. The ride home was silent.

George broke the silence, "You seem disturbed?"

"Sorry, George. I promise it's not you. I'm just very upset about something. I had a very disturbing phone call while in the restroom," she lied.

They arrived at Susan's residence. George was sympathetic. Susan stepped out of the car with hardly a word, and made her way to her door. George was not invited to follow, so he didn't bother.

She had hidden the note in her purse. She pulled it out and read it again. She briefly considered the situation and thought about her options as she changed into her nightgown. It was both surreal and scary. Obviously, someone who knew about Natasha's case had slipped her the note.

Her mind was flooded with questions. How in the hell could some stranger help with this situation? How could she possibly discuss a patient's case with anyone without violating HIPPA regulations? Why was the note slipped to her in the bathroom of that restaurant? Was she being stalked?

Although she didn't have much in the way of answers, she understood one thing. There was no way in hell she was going to e-mail this lady. That option was out of the question. She would get the MRI approved in 2 or 3 weeks after the insurance company had made their profit, period. That was it.

She calmed down over the next few hours. She called George and apologized. She invited him over to finish the evening off and he accepted. She made all the craziness of the evening worth his while. George was glad the pendulum had swung back the other way.

The next few days were filled with one emergency after the next. Dr. Harrison was very busy on call. She checked twice to see if the insurance company had called and she was not surprised to learn that there was no word from them yet. Then she got so occupied with tasks immediately at hand, that she momentarily forgot all about Natasha's case. She took a break for a few minutes and checked her personal e-mail.

The e-mail server was part of the large hospital systems service. If mail was from outside the system, permission had to be given to allow the mail through the securities filter to be seen. Drug companies and other entities were constantly bombarding the neurosurgeon with trash e-mails. Normally she ignored her junk mail, but this time she wanted to look through it because she had inadvertently trashed an important message sent to her by a friend. She clicked on the proper selection, and allowed the outside mail to be viewed. As she scanned the mail, she kept the arrow on delete, and trashed 30 drug company advertisements and offers for payment to fill out surveys. "What is this?" she exclaimed aloud.

The note in the bathroom was not a joke. I can help you with the problem at the insurance company. I understand if you do not want to talk. Just send me the patient's name, what is wrong with her, and the insurance company's name. I will take care of the problem anonymously.

Dr. Susan Harrison felt ill. When distressed, her language regressed even farther. "How in the hell did this crazy bitch get my e-mail address?" She swore loudly enough that her nurse, Lisa, hurried to the room.

"Dr. Harrison, what's the matter?" Lisa asked, with great concern. "You look pale." Lisa noticed that she was looking at something on her computer screen.

Dr. Harrison clicked the 'next message' selection, saving the anonymous note for further review. The doctor asked for a wet wash cloth, and was given one.

"I just read a very upsetting e-mail from a friend, and I need a minute."

Lisa closed the door and went back to her station. Dr. Harrison began to re-evaluate the situation. The anonymous note alone had not compelled her to respond, but with the addition of the e-mail, Dr. Harrison began to seriously contemplate the options.

Simply knowing which hospital she worked at would allow someone to take an educated guess at her e-mail address. The personal delivery of the note to her bathroom stall was actually more disturbing. What really caused Dr. Susan Harrison fear was the fact that someone had made such a concerted effort to persuade her to connect.

Between the fatigue from lack of sleep and the e-mail, she had trouble concentrating on her other patients as she continued her day. With great difficulty, she finished the day's work. After her paperwork was completed, she asked the nurse to complete one last task. She asked Lisa to draft a letter to the insurance company regarding Natasha Kapinski's MRI. She dictated the letter. It had a tone of desperation with a hint of sarcasm.

After everyone left the office, she grabbed a cup of coffee, and signed onto her e-mail again. "How could it hurt to reply to an e-mail?" she wondered aloud. She began to debate with herself. HIPPA was to be considered. She would be violating the privacy act by sharing the requested information with this unknown party. She looked at the sender's email address, ROBIN HOOD M.D. @ SPELLBOUND. NET. She checked the letter she received in the bathroom. It was the same e-mail as was on the letter.

Robbing the rich insurance companies, and giving to the poor patients. "Ha, ha!" she giggled. "Well, I'll be damned! It's Doctor Robin Hood!" For some reason, the name on the e-mail gave some credence to this anonymous figure. She was so scared after receiving the first letter that she had not thought about the name on the e-mail.

"I will tell him thank you for his interest, but it would be against the law to give out the requested information." She timidly clicked on the reply selection, and began to type the response. She selected send, and then stared at the computer for a full five minutes before leaving the office.

Normally, she allowed her e-mails to pile up over several days. However, the next morning she was eager to check her mail, and had arrived uncharacteristically early at the office to do so. Sleep would not be the proper term for what she had done the evening before. She had passed out from the retched fatigue that she had experienced, secondary to the busy trauma call she had taken on over the previous days. She felt like a different person that morning, arriving at her office after a solid ten hours of sleep. She signed on to her e-mail and noted three messages. Two were from within the hospital, and one was from outside. She read the two intra-hospital messages, and allowed the third to be delivered. It was from ROBIN HOOD.

I understand your concerns. Let's not let the patient die because of petty legal concerns. Please give me the information before it is too late!

Dr. Harrison tapped lightly on the keypads trying to think of a response.

HIPPA laws would be violated if I gave you a patient name and diagnosis. I could get fined or even go to jail. Thank you for your concern in the case.

Susan awaited the response. Fear had given way to intrigue. She thought, *Could some stranger really help get this MRI approved?* She had fluctuating feelings about the situation and had considered speaking to a colleague or even the police about it. Then she would consider: *What if Natasha has an aneurysm, and this Robin Hood lady is the only answer to our prayers? Maybe I shouldn't scare her off.*

A wave of rationalization began to flow through Dr. Harrison. She liked to write things down and look at them, instead of keeping the ideas captive in her head. Removing a notepad from her desk she made two columns. One was labeled plus and the other minus. She began to list out the pros and cons.

On the plus side she listed: Robin Hood may get the MRI done, seems capable, has detective skills, has had no problem getting me to interact with her, may save the patient's life.

On the negative side: This is dangerous. I could be giving private medical information to some stalker. I could lose my medical license, career, or life by interacting with this crazy person. What is this girl going to do anyway? How can anyone persuade a heartless insurance company to allow this study? They have already made up their minds to play the waiting game. If some stranger fires a verbal attack their way, this may in fact delay the study. The insurance companies are in 100% control of the situation. The patients and doctors are the hostages. If you anger someone holding you hostage, you may get hurt, and you never get what you want! *You can catch more flies with honey,* the doctor thought, and turned back to her list and scribbled: How does this lady know about this case anyway? This is very disturbing in and of itself. Why does this person care?

She looked over the long negative and short positive lists and came to a conclusion. Dr. Harrison verbalized her ruling, "Obviously, this person is well meaning; however, the last e-mail will be my final response to her. She'll only delay the MRI….anyway, she'll probably just cause more difficulty for me than I can risk."

Susan didn't look at any further outside e-mails. She hoped the insurance company would soon approve the study and all of this nonsense would be over. She made sure Lisa had sent the scathing letter to the insurance company. Dr. Harrison commanded, "Call Natasha and see how she's feeling. Remind her to go to the emergency room if she has any weakness or loss of feeling in her hands or legs."

Natasha's headaches were apparently steady, but were not increasing in intensity. Dr. Harrison had made Natasha an appointment with a neurologist in her group. He prescribed additional pain medication and agreed that she should have an MRI. She was unable to keep up with her assignments because the pain was so intense.

A week passed without any contact from Robin Hood. Dr. Harrison was sure the insurance company would soon have to give in and approve the MRI. The insurance company was well aware that, even after the approval had been given, another several days or weeks would pass before the study would actually be done. This was good news for the insurance company's interest bearing account. By the time the claim was actually paid, several months would go by.

The insurance company had a right to verify that the claim was accurate. A month after they received the claim for payment of the MRI, they would send out a questionnaire to the patient. An explanation of benefits would be sent showing that nothing had been paid on the claim because the insurance company was awaiting a response from the patient.

Cha-ching! …and the interest would roll in!

# CHAPTER SIX

"Mom, Dr. Harrison says she'll get the study approved. You heard her…" concluded Natasha, as she tried to calm her mother.

"Baby, you're so sick you're having trouble in school. You haven't had a day in weeks that was free from headaches!" cried Julie Kapinski. Her daughter had always made the honor roll and had always enjoyed studying and excelling in academic pursuits. It pained her to see her daughter so frustrated about falling behind in school. She knew it bothered Natasha as much as the pain itself. She wished she could take away the pain. She'd do anything to take her daughter's place in the suffering. So Julie Kapinski suffered right along with her daughter… but rather than physical pain, she suffered the emotional and mental anguish of not being able to do a thing about her daughter's suffering. But much, much worse was the growing anticipation of the cause of the pain…What if Natasha had a life-threatening condition and none of them knew it? What if she was only moments away from an emergency situation? What if she did have an aneurysm and they got to the ER too late? Julie shuddered and willed herself to stop herself in her tracks… No, she wouldn't go there. She couldn't. They were going to save her baby. That was all there was to it.

Natasha had been trying all along to hide her growing fear from her mother, but the pain was finally getting to be too much. Now, as her mom wrung her hands with worry, Natasha couldn't keep up the stiff upper lip any longer. "Mom," she wailed; "I've seen the other doctor, and he agrees that I need an MRI. Dr. Harrison has called and written letters to the insurance company and I've called the insurance company. There's been no response. I don't know what else to do!"

Mrs. Kapinski, with mouth set in a determined grimace, marched over to the kitchen phone and dialed the insurance company's customer service number and demanded: "I want to speak with the president of the company!"

"Ma'am, is there something I can help you with?" inquired the surly receptionist.

"I told you I want to speak with the president of the company, not some smart-ass secretary!" fired Natasha's mother.

"I'm not sure what's going on with you ma'am, but the CEO of D.J.S. insurance company does not take calls except by appointment. Are you a policy holder?" asked the unhelpful worker.

"No, but unfortunately my daughter is insured with you greedy bastards."

"Ma'am, is your daughter an adult?"

"Yes, she's an adult, but I still want to speak with the president, or as you call him, the CEO of your company. In the name of money, your company is denying my daughter the study that she desperately needs. I'm going to get this crap straightened out one way or another." Natasha's mother was now more determined than ever.

The receptionist continued to stonewall the irate mother. "I'm sorry but we are not permitted to talk to families of adult clients. Your daughter will need to call the 800 number herself."

Mrs. Kapinski screamed: "She has called you and you will not help her! I will sue….."

The receptionist slammed the receiver down while the client's mother was in mid-sentence. She turned to a co-worker and began to complain. "I am not going to listen to someone curse at me. She threatened to sue us. This idiot doesn't know you can't sue insurance companies. That woman was crazy as hell. I don't get paid enough to listen to this crap. What do you want for lunch?"

Real estate in metropolitan Atlanta was not cheap. In fact, it was damn expensive. D.J.S. insurance company did not balk at the cost. The new multi-story office building was a good investment. It made sense to showcase the powerful corporation to the public. When a corporation had a large physical presence, clients had increased confidence, albeit unwarranted, in the company. They purchased an old building in midtown and demolished it in order to make room for the new corporate headquarters.

The grand opening and ribbon-cutting ceremony was held in May of 1996. The 28 story, glass structure was a beautiful sight. On a sunny day, the blue luster blended into the blue sky. The two seemed to merge in a celestial embrace as you moved around the building, regardless of whether you backed away from it or came towards it.

As Julie Kapinski stood on the sidewalk looking up at the mega-million dollar structure, she began to understand what her daughter's premiums were actually subsidizing. She was amazed and disgusted at the size of the reception area alone. She entered the front door and pushed her way to the welcome desk.

"How may I help you?" asked the receptionist. Her forced smile quickly vanished as she recognized Mrs. Kapinski's voice.

"It seems that some very rude receptionist employed by this company hung up on me earlier today. As luck would have it, I was able to find the address of your corporate office. When I saw the address, I knew this was my day. I live about an hour away so I thought we could have a face to face chat."

The receptionist was stunned to be three feet away from the same crazy woman she thought she'd gotten rid of earlier that day. Gently, she slid her hand under the desk and hit a security 'call' button. She was trying to follow the guidelines for dealing with an irate customer. She'd learned the most effective methods to remain non-confrontational in the mandatory conflict resolution class the company had subsidized when she took the job. She tried not to make direct eye contact with the loud, red-faced woman in front of her. She neither smiled nor frowned.

"What I was trying to explain to you before I was so rudely cut off was that I will sue the hell out of you son of a bitches if anything happens to my daughter!" Julie Kapinski fumed.

Julie felt the presence of others around her. Two large security guards stepped up behind her and listened to the conversation.

Mrs. Kapinski continued despite the interruption. "I want to speak to the CEO of this company! I am not leaving until you assholes, you-- you greedy bastards, approve my daughter's MRI! She suffers with severe headaches every day and she may have an undiagnosed aneurysm!" She began to cry.

The demeanor of the receptionist changed after security help arrived. She now had a scowl on her face. She spoke around the now sobbing woman, directly to the two security guards. "I've explained to this lady that we can't talk to her because she's not a client, her daughter is. She's insisting on speaking to our CEO, but she doesn't have an appointment. When I asked her to have her daughter call the company, she became abusive over the telephone. Now, she's here behaving the same way. I feel threatened by her. Please remove her from the building."

Julie Kapinski had never been in a fight in her life. The larger of the two security guards approached her right arm, and lightly grasped it. He said in a firm, but convincing voice, "Ma'am, we're going to have to escort you out of the building." The smaller, but certainly still sizeable, guard reached for her left arm.

Julie Kapinski began to operate at a primitive level. Her daughter was going to die, and no one was going to help. Now, she was being thrown out of the one place where she could get help for her daughter. Her fight or flight mechanism was ignited with the grasp of the security guards. She chose the former.

She broke free of the physical restraint, jumped over the counter and landed on the receptionist. She began choking the receptionist and screaming nearly incomprehensible profanities as the security guards entered the fight. The normally civilized Mrs. Kapinski lashed out against the two large male security guards with the ferocity of a prize fighter defending his title. She was finally restrained. She had to be held, because the security guards did not have hand cuffs. The larger one screamed, "call 911, damn it! This woman is crazy!"

\* \* \*

"Sergeant, she has no criminal record. Her address checks out. We have a call into this doctor who she claims will be able to explain this whole mess to us," explained the perplexed deputy at the Fulton County Jail.

"I've seen some crazy shit, but this gets the award for the day," declared the duty sergeant. He stood at the one way mirror and observed the attractive, well-dressed lady sip her coffee, patting her lips daintily with a napkin. She looked like someone waiting to pick out a carpet color, not a violent criminal who needed to be pulled out of a brawl. According to the arresting officers, she had beaten the shit out of two burly security guards at an insurance company. In addition, she had assaulted a receptionist. When police arrived, 400 pounds of flesh was required to keep her on the ground, and the two security guards were begging for help.

"She must be schizophrenic. They can flip back and forth. They can go from passive to violent just like that," observed the deputy, snapping his fingers. "I used to see it all the time when I patrolled the southern district."

"Yeah, maybe so. I'll have the psychologist visit with her. There's something different about this, though. When I interviewed her, she didn't seem crazy. Mrs. Kapinski had a logical explanation for her violent behavior. She apologized for wasting the police department's time. I've never heard that from any of the nutcases we get in here. She told me her daughter was going to die because the insurance company wouldn't approve some type of medical study. She told me it was so frustrating, she just "lost it." It seems to me she was just a mother bear fighting for the life of her cub," the sergeant surmised. A phone rang in the office behind them, and the deputy picked up.

"This is Dr. Harrison, I was paged."

The deputy called for the sergeant to come to the telephone.

"Sergeant Johnson here. I'm sorry to bother you, Doctor, but we have a situation that needs some clarification." The sergeant notified Dr. Harrison about the arrest of Mrs. Kapinski. The doctor verified that the allegations that Mrs. Kapinski made against the insurance company were true.

"May I speak with Mrs. Kapinski?" asked the doctor.

"I suppose its okay, though she's in custody, and I am going to have to 'book' her tonight," the officer concluded.

"Dr. Harrison, I didn't mean to get into this mess! I'm just so scared about Natasha. I didn't know what I was doing. I went to the insurance company's headquarters because they wouldn't talk to me on the phone. I lost control," Julie Kapinski wailed to the doctor.

Susan Harrison was mortified at the thought that she may have inflamed the distraught mother to the point of violence. She thought back on the conversation in the office, and could not recall any specific remarks which could have caused this much anxiety. On the other hand, the fear of the unknown was a very powerful motivator. Natasha and Julie had likely conjured up the worst case scenario if the MRI wasn't done.

"I want you to calm down so we can talk this through. There's something I need to ask you," Dr. Harrison said in a calming voice.

After a few more sobs, Julie asked, "What is it?"

"I'm not sure I should even talk to you about this, but I was contacted by an anonymous person who said she could help with our situation." After pausing for a moment, Dr. Harrison continued. "I don't know this person, or what she is capable of; good or bad, but in light of today's events I need to ask if you're interested in talking to her."

Mrs. Kapinski whispered: "Hell yes, I'll talk to her. I'll talk to anybody if there's a chance they can help. How do I reach her?"

Dr. Harrison reiterated her disclaimer to Mrs. Kapinski and begrudgingly gave her the e-mail address.

The Kapinskis were notified of Julie's arrest and quickly preceded to the police station to bail Julie out. Hardly a word was spoken on the way home. The family was in utter disbelief of Julie's radical actions. Just as Mr. Kapinski thought that the day could not get more bizarre, Julie asked, "How do I send and receive an e-mail on a computer?"

# CHAPTER SEVEN

———•❧•———

"I can't breath. Stop it! You're gonna kill me!" cried the CEO.

"That is the plan, my friend," explained the assailant.

A noose was around the neck of Jim (Jimbo) Simmons, the Chief Executive Officer of D.J.S. Insurance Company. He had awoken in the current predicament, not knowing where he was or what was going on. It was pitch black. He was terrified. His hands were tied behind his back. A hood or sac seemed to be covering his head. A threatening voice would make some comment to him, and then he would choke for a few minutes. His head was killing him because of the intermittent asphyxia.

"Do you have a headache?" asked the attacker in a sadistic tone.

"Yes, I have a headache!"

"How would you like to have headaches like this one all the time?" asked the attacker.

Jim coughed, now choking on saliva and tears, "please stop!"

"Buddy, I asked you a question and I expect an answer!"

The CEO was thrown roughly to the floor. A knee dug in the middle of his back and the noose around his neck was tightened. His neck was jerked upwards as the rope was yanked by the assailant. Jim Simmons began to fight for his life. He kicked and rolled and was strangled for a full minute. It seemed like an hour to him. The captor released the CEO and retreated.

Jim Simmons knew that all men were appointed death. He thought of his baptism as a child, and reflected on his impending death. *Had he lived a good enough life to go to Heaven? What would be said at his eulogy?*

Jim heard a door open and footsteps moving in his direction. He didn't move a muscle. He felt the presence of another person near him.

The silence was broken. "Do you have an answer to my question?"

"I would not care to have this much pain every day, sir," Jim replied.

Like an injured animal awaiting a merciful last blow to end the pain, the CEO awaited the end. But to his surprise, no more punishment came. The CEO was placed in a chair and his hands were freed. His mask was ripped off and Jim closed his eyes for fear of what he would see.

"Open your eyes," demanded the kidnapper.

Jim shook his head slowly from left to right, eyes still squeezed shut.

"If you do not open your eyes, I will be forced to surgically remove your eyelids. Would I need prior approval from your insurance company to do this procedure?"

"Please don't hurt me anymore," pleaded the CEO as he opened his left eyelid a crack, and then followed with the right one. His fear was affirmed, as a large figure wearing camouflage clothing and a ski mask came into view. He was standing directly in front of the CEO. The thick arms of the masked man were crossed over each other like brawny sailor's knots. He glared down at the CEO with cold, steely, almost reptilian eyes. Jim squinted at the muscled forearms of his captor, and was reminded of the massive tow ropes on the big ships that docked at the wharf around the bay from his summer home. He was suddenly very conscious of his own skinny arms. It'd been his New Year's resolution for the past six years to start working out at the gym. He never seemed to get around to it…too busy making money. And now he couldn't have defended himself against this thug if his life depended on it. *Shit!* he thought. *My life does depend on it! Oh, shit! Oh shit, oh shit, oh shit, oh shit! I'm going to die. And I haven't finished writing my will. And no one knows where I am. My wife is going to have to identify my body when they find me…if they find me. And my daughter…*He choked back a sob. *My daughter won't have a daddy. This can't be happening. This can't be happening. Holy shit; I've been kidnapped and I'm going to die.*

For a long spell the masked man didn't say a word and the CEO had ample time to continue working himself into a state of panic. In fact, the kidnapper barely flexed a muscle. The only movement Jim detected was what looked like a subtle grinding of his teeth behind the mask, but he couldn't be sure. Finally, the masked man broke the silence. He turned on a video projector and directed the CEO to look at the screen which lowered on the wall to his right.

"The health insurance industry has struck again. In order to save your company money, and to increase your personal profits, you are denying this young lady the care she needs."

A recent picture of Natasha Kapinski was shown on the screen.

"She suffers from severe headaches every single day. Thanks to D.J.S. insurance company, her doctor is not being permitted to find out exactly why she has these headaches. Since you are profiting from her suffering, I wanted to point out to you how unacceptable your behavior is. You have suffered minimally today compared to the pain that this young lady endures on a routine basis. She may, in fact be in danger of dying. Her doctor is not even able to tell her whether she's currently in danger!

The slide changed to show the Atlanta headquarters of D.J.S. insurance company. The next picture was the luxurious home and then the private yacht owned by "Jimbo" Simmons.

"The bible says, 'Where your treasure lies, so does your heart.' It's obvious to me where your heart is."

The CEO trembled at the biblical quotation. He was sure that this psychopath was going to kill him at any moment.

"Are you interested in having a chance to live?"

"I don't want to die! Please! I'll give you anything you want."

"If you're willing to make amends for you and your company's indecorous behavior, I will give you an opportunity to leave here alive."

The use of proper language and a sophisticated tone unnerved the CEO even more. It just didn't fit the violent situation. Although he was a college graduate, he was not exactly sure what was meant by the words used by the madman, but he certainly understood the life and death situation that he was in.

Jim sheepishly replied, "I'm sorry for what I've done. I'll help the girl in any way I can."

"If you promise to have her MRI approved by tomorrow, I will let you live. In addition, you will anonymously donate $150,000 of your own money to a local homeless shelter. I want D.J.S. insurance company to begin a community outreach program for troubled teens.

You will provide alternative programs for kids in order to deter gang involvement."

The CEO was asked to read a statement and did so. As if he wasn't convinced of the danger that he and his family were in, the captor made further threats against Jim's family if he breathed a word about the kidnapping to anyone. Jim assured the masked man that he would never utter a word.

He was relieved when the kidnapper blindfolded him and guided him into the back seat of a car idling outside. Jim's captor dropped him off at the curb 2 blocks away from his hundred million dollar home. 'Jimbo' Simmons willed himself to walk back to his house in his usual cocky stride, even though his knees felt so much like Jell-O that he wasn't sure his legs would even continue to hold up his body.

"Daddy, where's your car?" his 13-year-old daughter, Danielle, called to him as he came up their cobbled limestone driveway, panting from exertion. She and her best friend Sarah were just climbing into the back seat of the convertible he had given her for her 13th birthday. Since she was a few years from being able to drive, he had given her a chauffeur as well. He felt that owning a good car was paramount to success in the world. He wanted the best for his daughter. He wanted her to have every head start possible. For Danielle, it was an odd sight to see her dad walk up the driveway; almost as odd as it would have been to see a UFO land in their yard. Ridiculous as it was, her father tried to act as if it was the most natural thing in the world to be huffing up the driveway in his three-piece suit.

"I thought --thought I'd --wanted to get --a little exercise," he huffed, trying to catch his breath.

"Whatever!" Danielle retorted. As the butler opened the front door for Jim and he stepped inside the vestibule, he overheard Danielle remarking to her friend, "Parents are so weird sometimes!"

\*     \*     \*

"Dr. Harrison, there's a telephone call for you from Natasha Kapinski's insurance company," shouted the front office clerk over the office intercom.

"What in the hell is going to be their excuse today?" Dr. Harrison crowed as she was handed the receiver.

Dr. Susan Harrison stood with a look of disbelief on her face, as she listened to the words she'd been yearning to hear for so long. She hardly spoke a word in return as she listened to the reviewer declare Natasha eligible for the MRI. She copied down the confirmation number and passed the telephone receiver back over the counter to the clerk.

She wondered aloud, "I wonder what made them change their minds so abruptly?"

As she was asking for Natasha's number, it hit her. *Robin Hood M.D.!*

"No way!" she breathed.

"Ma'am," answered her nurse.

"I'm sorry, I was thinking out loud."

"May I speak with Natasha, please?" Dr. Harrison decided to make the call herself. This family needed some good news.

"She's in terrible pain, I was about to call you and see if we needed to come to the emergency room," answered Julie Kapinski.

Dr. Harrison was dying to ask Julie if she had sent any e-mail correspondence to Robin Hood but decided to take care of her daughter's medical situation first and foremost.

"Bring her to the MRI area in the x-ray department as quickly as possible," ordered Dr. Harrison. "The insurance company called and they've approved the study."

"Robin Hood said he could help," shrieked Julie Kapinski excitedly. "He did it! He got those bastards to approve my baby's study. He did it!"

"She did it," corrected Dr. Harrison.

"What?" asked the jubilant mother, momentarily confused.

"Never mind, just get her here."

Dr. Harrison declared an emergency in radiology and made arrangements for Natasha to have an emergency MRI of the brain.

The Pavlovian response to the sound of a beeper is intrinsic to doctors. Pavlov's dog salivated at the sound of a bell, because this represented an association between food and a bell. Doctors curse at the sound of a beeper, because the beeping sound is associated with a sleepless night. One of Dr. Harrison's colleagues had noticed that Susan cursed every time her beeper went off. The colleague wisely suggested that she change the ring tone to something more soothing. Susan couldn't believe it, but it actually worked...for a time. Of course, as soon as she was conditioned to the new tone, her beeper began to again ignite involuntary cursing.

*RING, RING, RING!* "Damn it, what now!" Susan scolded the pager emitting the soft ringing sound. She looked at the number, and her pulse started to slow back down again as she realized that the emergency room was not paging her for another admission to the hospital. She did not recognize the number which was a good sign. She reached for her cell phone and dialed the number.

"Dr. Harrison, Dr. Nobil needs to speak to you right now!" exclaimed the x-ray technician.

"This girl has a very large aneurysm. I'm seeing edema in the surrounding tissue, and there's already a small amount of hemorrhage in the surrounding areas," the radiologist concluded.

"So, as I had expected, she has a bleeding aneurysm. It is a damn wonder she's still alive. Thank you for reading this so quickly. I'll call the operating room. I will sure as heck get the patient to the hospital right now!"

Dr. Harrison quickly dialed the operating room supervisor. Since the hospital where Dr. Harrison practiced was a trauma center, the operating room had protocols for the various levels of emergencies. She labeled Natasha's case the absolute highest priority and she was on the operating table within ten minutes.

*   *   *

"She should do just fine. I placed clips around the aneurysm which stopped the bleeding. Only a small amount of blood was present and I saw no damage to her brain tissue. Literally, this was found just in the nick of time. "There was a ninety-five percent chance she would have died in a couple of hours."

Julie Kapinski collapsed into Dr. Harrison's arms at the news. Her body could not handle any more stress. Cold wash cloths were placed on her face as she lay on the waiting room floor. She was trying to say something, but was whispering so softly that Dr. Harrison had to lean to the floor to hear her.

"Thank you Robin," Julie coughed and began to sob. "Thank you, Robin Hood!"

Mr. Kapinski made a queer face and looked at Dr. Harrison, "did she say Robin Hood?"

Dr. Harrison smiled to herself as she walked out of the waiting room. She could not help but wonder what in the hell this Robin Hood lady had said to the insurance company.

# CHAPTER EIGHT

"Gentlemen, you have to break a few eggs to make an omelet!" Jeffrey Warren, the key note speaker began. "Everywhere that we turn, more and more criticism is heaped on our industry's doorstep. Is it warranted? I think not! Most industries are applauded for cost reduction. We, on the other hand, are seen as villains for trying to maintain reasonable costs. We are scolded for requiring even the slightest trace of a certification processes prior to an expensive study. Other industries are congratulated for quality assurance."

Applause broke out at the Saturday evening meeting of the National Association of Health Insurance Executives. It was obvious that the speaker was getting a rush out of the heightened energy in the auditorium. Cocktails, before and after dinner, had been consumed. The annual meeting was held this year in Orlando, Florida. The participants were also drunk from a full day of drinking booze while soaking up the sun at the hotel's pool. As the evening rambled on, a mob mentality settled even further over the inebriated crowd. Anything less than a rallying type speech would have been too subtle to be appreciated at this point in the evening.

The speaker bumped his own energy level up a few notches for his finale. "Some want us extinct!" he continued, pausing for dramatic effect. "They want a national health insurance program. It wasn't that long ago that some of our socialist comrades in congress proposed just that. The drum, ladies and gentlemen, is starting to beat again for the same nonsense!"

"Boo, hiss!" shouted members of the audience.

"Oh yes, they want us gone! We are the enemy!'

"No! They're the enemy! We're the good guys!" screamed an intoxicated CFO from the back of the auditorium.

A great roar of laughter erupted from the audience. The speaker took a drink of water and waited for the last titters to quiet down before gravely admitting, "There is no doubt that the health insurance industry has its public relations difficulties."

The speaker stepped away from the podium and a screen was lowered. A video began to play.

"Who is filling your prescriptions?" A pharmacist holding a medication bottle was walking towards the camera. "More and more frequently, when a doctor writes your prescription, the insurance company will change your medication. Why? In order for the insurance company to make more money! If your lucky, medicines are changed to equivalent medications, but other times they are only a close proximity. Always, the cheaper medications are used. While we support generic drug use, changing a drug to an entirely different medication should be left to the discretion of the prescribing physician and pharmacist. We, at the National Association of Better Pharmaceutical Practices, believe that insurance companies should not be making these decisions!"

The video continued for a total of a minute. Theodore Bexley leaned over to Jonathan Willingham and whispered: "Would you listen to this whiny bastard?!! Next he'll be wiping his tears on his lab coat!"

Jonathan responded in kind, "Before long, they'll be making commercials with orphans on the street wearing rags. They'll be claiming their insurance company caused them to lose their fortune."

The two executives's shared a laugh as the video ended and the speaker resumed.

"This is just the beginning of a media campaign that's being launched against us. As the drum for change begins to beat, our old enemies will emerge crying for a national health care system. I'm sure you all remember this cry on the evening news..." The speaker cupped his hands around his mouth and pitched his head upwards. He screamed, "40 MILLION UNINSURED PATIENTS! WE HAVE

A HEALTH CARE CRISIS! WE NEED A NATIONAL HEALTH CARE SYSTEM!"

Jimbo Simmons turned to his colleague seated to his right: "What they always fail to do is finish the sentence. Forty million people a year roll the dice and CHOOSE not to buy health insurance. It's only when they lose the bet they cry foul!"

Onstage, Jeffery Warren continued, "The United States spends more on healthcare by a huge magnitude than any other developed country. Who writes the checks?" he held his hand to his ear awaiting a response from the audience.

"We do," shouted a CEO from the third row.

"But, you see nobody looks at it that way," the speaker responded now driving his point home. "We have to change the public's perception of our industry and redirect the rage towards the greedy hospitals and doctors where it belongs. I had a procedure done as an outpatient this year. I was in the hospital for 8 hours and the bill was $37,000 dollars." The speaker repeated the figure slowly for effect. "Thirty-seven thousand dollars!"

"He must have had a penis pump put in for that price," slurred Theodore to his buddy Jimbo.

"I wouldn't pay $37,000 for an implantable vagina for my personal use only," Jimbo retorted.

Snorting and coughing on a mouth full of beer, Theodore laughed and slapped Jimbo on the back. "Damn, you're a crazy fool, Jimbo!" A couple of people in front of the two turned and glared to show their displeasure at the outburst.

"We need to show the public how good they actually have it," the speaker continued. "I propose that we do ads showing patients who have traveled to the United States to have elective surgery from Canada. In the Canadian system, patients have to get on a waiting list if they want non-emergency surgery. We can highlight a patient who would have been out of work three months waiting for surgery if they had not traveled to the United States. We can emphasize that it was more economical for the patient to pay for the surgery."

Jeffrey Warren was sounding more and more like a Southern Baptist preacher at a revival as he preached, "The truth about the quality of care received in national health systems needs to be exposed. In one Japanese clinic highlighted on American network news, the care was free but the doctor saw 150 patients in eight hours. Numbers were assigned to each patient upon arrival at the clinic and they were herded through like cattle at an auction! I hardly imagine that patients were given ample time for discussion of their medical case in that setting! Americans are accustomed to better care than this. Americans *deserve* better care than this! Louis Sullivan was quoted as saying, 'a government-run healthcare system will have the efficiency of the post office and the compassion of the Internal Revenue Service.' Take a look at the Veteran's Administration healthcare system. The patients tolerate an immobilizing bureaucracy in order to get their medications for free. You don't have to look far to find story after story in the media about the horrible care that VA patients receive. Many of them use the private healthcare sector for physician care and see the government doctors to receive prescriptions only. Is this what we want for all Americans? I think not!" The audience rumbled in agreement.

"Also, we need to showcase our success stories. We all have patients alive today because of our products. How many patients are survivors because we pay for pap smears, mammograms, and colonoscopies? We lose millions of dollars paying for screening studies but do it anyway because it's the right thing to do! And let's not forget to point out to the public a very important fact: Insurance companies provide the level of service purchased by the employer. If an employer wishes to purchase certain more expensive services, such as one paying for any medication that a doctor writes no matter how cost ineffective we will sell them the plan.

The speaker continued, "We hire nurse educators, physicians, and pharmacists to make sure our clients receive the highest quality of care. In the near future, we're even going to grade our doctors on their performances. If they do not have our diabetic and hypertensive patients at goal levels of blood pressure and blood sugar, we will reduce reimbursement. This will make quality care an incentive and hold the doctors accountable."

"We will fight the illegal price-fixing activities of Physician/Hospital organizations. We are working diligently with Congress to ensure that the anti-trust laws are enforced in medicine. Many doctors and hospitals feel that they are above the law." The audience murmured in agreement.

"Another issue is the price of prescription drugs in the United States! We pay more for medications in the United States than any other country does. The pharmaceutical companies entice doctors to prescribe these expensive new drugs by buying their favor. Who pays for it? We do!"

The speaker concluded: "it is only fair to outline the amount of fraud that occurs in medical billing. This is an appropriate counter-attack. Millions of dollars in fines are levied each year by government agencies against doctors and hospitals. These medical personnel are criminals. Over-billing, under documentation, services not provided, fabricated patient cases, workers compensation scams… these are just a few of the crimes which doctors are being fined and imprisoned for. Once the public learns the truth we will be vindicated!"

Without any further fanfare, Jeffrey Warren turned and walked off the stage. He received loud applause for a job well done.

The moderator arrived at the podium, and the applause subsided. "We all need to have a good laugh every now and then. Our next speaker is a medical doctor with a keen sense of humor. He takes the notion of laughter being the best medicine to the extreme. He's written a hilarious book about his medical school and residency training. Dr. Jones has been featured on the *Tonight Show and David Letterman*. Let's welcome our funny doctor, Dr. Hall Jones."

Dr. Jones made his way to the podium as the applause continued. As it began to die down, he grasped the microphone and tapped it quizzically a few times before speaking.

"After that speech, I feel like a turkey invited to Thanksgiving dinner. I was interviewing a patient the other day as she lay on the stretcher in the emergency room. I asked her how long she had been bed-ridden. She replied, *'Honey, my husband has been dead for years.'*" The audience exploded into a chorus of inebriated guffaws.

Spurred by the laughter, the doctor continued: "Has anyone in here ever done anything embarrassing? I want you to think about your most embarrassing moments. I have a few unfortunately. I looked in a 50-year-old female patient's throat and saw how bad it looked. As I continued the examination, I couldn't think of anything else. I put my stethoscope on her chest and instead of asking her to take a deep breath, I told her to take a deep throat! She turned to look at me and said with a straight face, 'Doc, I've seen that movie!' Guys, I wanted to find a hole to crawl in," Dr. Jones laughed.

"There is lot of miscommunication in medicine. When you combine complex medical terminology and hearing impairment, you create some funny situations. I had my nurse call a patient and tell him that we were going to put him on a pain patch. He was so angry that he drove to the office in a huff and demanded to see me. I could see the anger on his face and I asked him what was wrong. He huffed: *'I don't care if you are a doctor. I'm not smoking a crack pipe for anybody. That stuff is bad for you.'*"

"And then there was a little old lady in a wheelchair who was contemplating the name of the medication which another doctor had prescribed. She thought and thought and then recalled the name of the medication. *'Viagra!'* she loudly concluded. I looked down at her chart trying not to laugh. Snickers broke out in the room. Her daughter leaned over and explained to her what Viagra was. *'Good God! I'm too old for that!'* she replied, glancing shyly in my direction."

"Add a language barrier to the mix, and it gets really interesting. I was trying to transfuse a Hispanic gentlemen in the Intensive Care Unit, so I arranged a 3-way call between the patient, interpreter, and myself. As I explained the risks and benefits of the blood transfusion, I noticed that the patient had the international look of horror on his face. This needed no interpretation. The patient made a two minute plea to the interpreter, and then the interpreter queried me, *'Senior Lopez wishes to know why you wish to drain all the blood from his body...'*"

"Doctors and nurses have difficulty with communication also. I was delivering a baby while I was in residency when a rookie nurse technician and I had a funny miscommunication. The delivery had stalled and I asked for a vacuum to assist in delivering the baby. Now, anyone in obstetrics knows that a vacuum is an instrument used to assist in the delivery of the baby's head. This technician didn't move so I turned and asked her a second time, 'Would you please bring me the vacuum?' She left the room and returned pushing a Hoover vacuum cleaner!"

After the laughter began to subside, the comedian continued. "One of my colleagues in obstetrics had sent home a lady who was pregnant with her first child. She had contractions, but her cervix had not yet begun to dilate. This is very common with the first pregnancy. The first child usually comes into the world very slowly. My friend reassured the patient's very large and mean-looking husband that the delivery would be in a few days. Thirty minutes after sending the patient home, the doctor received an emergency message in his beeper. *Delivery in the emergency room parking lot. Come ASAP....* The doctor grabbed an emergency delivery kit and proceeded to the parking lot. In the back seat of a 1985 LTD lay his patient delivering her first son. Her husband was trying to assist the nurses. He explained to the nurses: *'The doctor just saw her and told us it would be a few days before she delivered. I guess he was wrong!'* The doctor faced the snarling husband and finished the delivery. The baby was fine and all ended well. One hour after the delivery, the doctor's beeper rang again. *Delivery in the lobby!* The overweight doctor screamed a profanity and grabbed an emergency delivery kit. He retrieved his medical student and proceeded down four flights of stairs. He entered the lobby, and looked around. He didn't see anyone in labor. In fact, the only person in the lobby was the lady sitting at the reception desk. Perplexed, the doctor and student, both winded after the run, proceeded to the desk. *'I was paged for a delivery in the lobby. Where's the delivery?'* the doctor asked. The receptionist reached behind her and retrieved a box of candy and a flower arrangement. *'Happy Father's Day!'* the receptionist announced. The doctor's wife had sent him the gift."

"I grew up in a rural area and I've practiced there for almost 20 years. I much prefer it. We have our own language, and we're very proud of it. However, this does lead to difficulties when communicating with the outside world. Sometimes, something as simple as filling out a medical questionnaire is challenging for we country folks. One of my patients wrote the word *RETARD* as the answer to her occupation. In rural Georgia, that's just the proper pronunciation for 'retired.' In my town, if you're tired, you're *'Tard.'* A hysterectomy is a *History correction.* Spinal meningitis becomes *Spine of many Jesus.* A rotator cuff repair is a *Rotary cap repair.* Spinal canal stenosis is *spark plug stereo. I've lost my gumption* means I have fatigue (folks, that's another word for *tard, by the way*). I've had to learn to decipher the rural version of every medication name. *'Arangatang'* is what one of my patients calls his Atacand. I have another lady who refers to her Humalog as her *'Humor log.'* One of my patients misunderstood the directions on the stool collection card kit. The instructions on the kit said to sample three separate bowel movements. The patient called my nurse asking her if he could PLEASE go to the bathroom. He told her that he was not going to do any more tests that required him not to have a bowel movement for three days.

That just hurt too bad!" The audience hooted and howled, slapping their thighs and guffawing into their napkins.

"Well, that's about all I've got up my sleeve tonight folks," Dr. Jones concluded. "Thank you guys for having me here to speak. I know y'all are here for serious business, but I hope you don't forget to have a little fun as well. You know what they say ---A laugh a day keeps the doctor away! And I know y'all definitely want to keep those doctors away, huh?!!!"

The room erupted in loud applause. Dr. Jones had a proud grin on his face as he left the stage. He thought the evening's routine had gone very well. These insurance guys were an easy crowd to work, as long as he didn't go too hard on the industry. It was usually a tougher crowd at medical conventions, but he could always get the doctors to loosen up by taking a particularly nasty jab at the insurance industry. For the doctors, he'd always begin with an insurance joke: "What's the difference between an insurance policy and a pickled herring? The herring doesn't stink as bad when the heat is on!"

Dr. Jones himself wasn't crazy about the workings of the medical system but neither was he dedicated to changing it. In fact, the national insurance and pharmaceutical conventions held in Las Vegas, Florida, California, and Hawaii every year were his bread and butter. As long as big companies continued to pay his fat speaker's honorarium and put him up in the executive suites of 4 star hotels, he didn't mind what they did. And he enjoyed the celebrity status in his niche of the entertainment world.

The boorishly drunken executives patted him on the back and shook his hand as he came offstage and headed back to his hotel suite to sink into his fluffy bed to channel-surf and nurse a tall scotch and soda. It was a good life. He received all of the perks and all he had to do was make people laugh. No pressure to rush through procedures to get to the next patient, no anxieties about malpractice suites, no worrying about whether he was making the correct diagnosis or prescribing the right medications…he was happy not to be in practice any longer. It was a good life, a comfortable life, and it suited him just fine.

\* \* \*

"I played golf with this guy in Hawaii who was Japanese. He spoke only four words in English: 'shit' and 'out of bounds,'" Jimbo said as he walked towards the tee box.

Jimbo Simmons, Theodore Bexley, Jonathan Willingham, and Brad(Skip) Omins were gathered in a 'foursome' for a round of golf on the last day of the conference. Even though it was only 9:30 am, it was already getting muggy. It was looking like Jimbo would likely maintain the 'honors' of first off the tee all day, since he was by far the best golfer in the group. He hit his drive 275 yards in the middle of the fairway.

"You like that one?" Jimbo turned to the group and asked rhetorically.

"Prick!" replied Theodore under his breath.

To no one's surprise and to the expectations of Jimbo Simmons, the winner for the day with a round of 72 was Jim 'Jimbo' Simmons. Skip came in second with a 78, Jonathan suffered through with an 89, and Theodore, having a tougher day than usual, shot a 101.

"You were in the woods more than a lumberjack!" Jimbo poked at his suffering golf partner.

"Fuck you!" Theodore retorted.

"Hey guys, let's get something to eat," Jonathan summoned the group.

The 19th hole was a bar and restaurant located in the club house. The four men sat down for a meal. They ate hardily and ordered a round of drinks.

"Guys, you know I'm worried about our industry's public image. I had a guy get really upset at me about someone's procedure not being paid for," Jonathan began.

Theodore and Jimbo each paused mid-bite.

Skip chimed in: "Hell, we have people get pissed off all the time. I wouldn't worry about that. What happened?"

"It was nothing," Jonathan lied: "He was just really angry. I guess I'm just not used to dealing directly with the public. He was really pissed off though. He scared me, to be honest with you."

Theodore Bexley and Jimbo Simmons both avoided eye contact with the others at the table.

"Well, let me tell you boys, I will be hitting the driving range and I will beat all your asses next year," Theodore joked, trying to change the subject.

# CHAPTER NINE

Timothy Sims was doing very well. The bone marrow transplant had worked wonderfully and he had made a remarkable recovery. He continually received glowing letters of encouragement. He loved mail time. It was his job to retrieve and open the mail every day. On this particular day the first envelope he opened didn't have a return address, but didn't have the appearance of junk mail. He didn't think anything of it until he opened it and began to read.

TO: TIMOTHY SIMS, DEBRA JUSTIN, AND NATASHA KAPINSKI,

IT IS NO MISTAKE THAT YOU THREE ARE ALIVE AND WELL TODAY. IT IS BECAUSE OF DRASTIC ACTIONS TAKEN AGAINST THE CHIEF EXECUTIVE OFFICERS OF YOUR INSURANCE COMPANIES THAT THE DECISION WAS MADE FOR YOU TO HAVE YOUR TREATMENT OR MEDICATION PAID FOR. THIS DRASTIC ACTION INCLUDED THE THREAT OF DEATH TO THE CEO. IF HE DID NOT ALLOW THE PROCEDURE OR MEDICATION TO BE PAID FOR, HE WAS GOING TO PAY WITH HIS LIFE. ALL OF THE CEOs DECIDED TO LIVE.

IT IS TIME FOR YOU TO RETURN THE FAVOR. I WANT YOU TO MAKE PUBLIC THE CIRCUMSTANCES THAT LED UP TO YOUR NEAR DEATH EXPERIENCE AT THE HANDS OF YOUR INSURANCE COMPANY. I WANT YOU TO PARTICIPATE IN A PRESS CONFERENCE WHICH I HAVE ARRANGED FOR YOU. ALL THREE OF YOU WILL BE PARTICIPANTS, AS YOU EACH HAVE HAD A SIMILAR CIRCUMSTANCE. I EXPECT YOU TO DO THE RIGHT THING AND MAKE PUBLIC THE ATROCITIES WHICH THE INSURANCE COMPANIES ARE COMMITTING AGAINST PATIENTS. YOU CAN SAVE OTHER PATIENTS' LIVES BY TELLING YOUR STORY. I SAVED THREE LIVES. YOU CAN SAVE THOUSANDS OF LIVES BY STEPPING UP TO THE PLATE.

## ROBIN HOOD M.D.

"Mom! Mom!" Timothy screamed.

Saurina Sims dropped the laundry and ran out to the kitchen to her son, her heart racing. Though her son was doing so much better, Saurina was constantly on pins and needles fearing a relapse and fearing that Tim's recovery was all just a happy dream that was about to end. "What is it?"

"Read this, Mom."

"Oh, my God!" Saurina gasped. "Oh, my God!"

\*   \*   \*

Debra Justin was feeling well. Her blood sugar was running in the normal range. She had not been ill once since she had resumed her long-acting insulin. Her primary care physician was elated. She was working full time and had applied to technical school. Since she lived in an apartment, she had a post office box. She checked her mail when she remembered to, usually two to three times weekly. This was one of those days. She threw her mail on the table...mostly bills and circulars. A large envelope caught her attention. Her name was written in a large typed font using capital letters. In the left hand upper corner the words ROBIN HOOD M.D. were typed.

"What the hell is this?" Debra screamed aloud as she read the contents of the letter.

\* \* \*

"Natasha, baby, you have mail," Julie Kapinski called.

"What is it? I am trying to study."

"I have no idea. Did you sign up for some type of Robin Hood book club? The sender is Robin Hood M.D.."

Natasha and her mother stood looking at the envelope.

"I haven't joined anything I can remember, but you know I did have my skull cracked open 6 months ago, and some of my memories may have leaked out." Natasha joked, making a waving motion over the top of her head.

Julie Kapinski began to hyperventilate and clutch her chest.

"Mom, what is it? What is wrong with you?"

"Robin Hood M.D., Robin Hood."

"Mom I can see that, but what's the matter with you?"

"Bring me a glass of water." Mrs. Kapinski gasped as she picked up the unopened envelope and sunk to the couch.

"Are you okay? Are you sick or something?"

"Baby, there's something I have to tell you. I didn't think, I mean, I didn't expect to ever hear from Robin Hood again."

"Mom, I hate to be blunt, but have you lost your mind once and for all? You're talking about fictional characters as if they're real and having a panic attack. Do I need to call a doctor?"

"Natasha, do you recall how the insurance company had a sudden change of heart and allowed your MRI to be done when it looked as though there was no way it was going to happen?"

"I was there, aneurysm and all!"

"Dr. Harrison gave me an anonymous person to contact by e-mail who said they could help us."

"That's why you got so interested in e-mail all of the sudden?"

"I gave your information to the stranger via e-mail. Within a few days, the insurance company had changed their mind."

Natasha sat down gently next to her mother.

Julie held up the envelope and pointed at the left, upper corner.

"Robin Hood M.D. is the 'name' of the person I was corresponding with."

Julie brushed Natasha's hair back from her face absently with tears welling up in her eyes.

"So he's not dangerous, right Mom? He helped us. I mean, you don't think this 'Robin Hood' guy would try to blackmail us or anything, right Mom? Right?"

Julie looked at her daughter helplessly but didn't answer. Natasha stared back at her mom. Silence encompassed the two.

"Let me open it, Mom."

# CHAPTER TEN

"Did you see this?" Samantha Huet slapped the paper down on the desk in front of Editor John Bartol, right on top of the stack of memos he was distractedly sifting through while poring over the emails on his computer.

"What is it?" snapped the overworked Lifestyles and Human Interest editor at the Atlanta Journal and Constitution. Ms. Huet knew enough not to interrupt him with petty stories at this time of the day.

"It's a press release for a news conference tomorrow at noon."

"Now Samantha, I know you're a rookie reporter and you don't yet have the power of discernment, but we get a hundred of these a week. Some jackass writes his first bad novel, thinks he's the next Hemmingway, and we get a press release about it like its 'big news!' People just don't know what it takes to make a newsworthy story! It's the one thing that hasn't changed in this business in thirty damn years!"

Ms. Huet persisted as the editor looked back at his computer screen. "I really think you should take a look at this, sir. I'm definitely going to this press conference! It'd be a big mistake for us to miss out on it."

John Bartol slowly turned his chair back around to face the reporter and sighed, "Let me have it."

The editor began to read and stood up from his chair. "Shit, will you look at this!"

Samantha rolled her eyes in disgust. She knew the apology she was due would never come from this dinosaur.

"I want full coverage. Call the Biltmore and make certain we have access before the doors open to the other press. I want front row seating. I want a reporter to do a story on each one of these patients. I also want the CEOs of each insurance company to be interviewed. Get moving!" John picked up the handset and began barking instructions into the receiver.

Samantha strolled out the door and cracked a grin. "One hundred per week my ass!"

*   *   *

"Sam, why do we have to arrive for a noon press conference at 9:30 am?" the photographer protested.

"Read this!" Samantha handed the photographer the press release.

## PRESS RELEASE

*I have kidnapped the CEOs of three health insurance companies, and made them pay for their heinous business decisions. I held one at gunpoint, strangled one, and poisoned the other, until they promised to change their ways. I will personally continue to put the life of every health insurance CEO in the country in jeopardy until they stop putting their clients' lives at risk. I am already planning the next kidnapping. Any CEO preventing a patient from getting proper care is risking their own life.*

*Natasha Kapinski, Timothy Sims, and Debra Justin would all be dead today if I had not taken drastic action against the Chief Executive Officers of their health insurance companies. They are alive today because of my interference.*

*You are invited to meet them and hear their stories at noon, January 7, 2014 at the Biltmore Hotel in downtown Atlanta, Ga.*

*Robin Hood M.D.*

"Holy shit, Let's get going!" the photographer exclaimed gleefully, eyes bulging with excitement. "I want front row seats for this thing!"

The area in front of the hotel was littered with reporters as they arrived. It was only 9:15 am. "I guess the word is out," Samantha sighed. "Damn it, I guess we'll have to fight our way to the front."

Luckily, many of the reporters were busy gathering gear from their trucks. Nate was able to run ahead of Samantha and scavenge two front row seats. He was told to protect these with his life. All the major media players were present. The room was abuzz with apprehension of the juicy upcoming press conference.

Natasha, Timothy, and Debra entered the conference room at different times and took their seats at the front. Twenty microphones were arranged at the podium, each labeled with the network symbol. Cameras lined the back of the room.

Robin Hood had given written instructions regarding the procedure for the press conference. Natasha was given instructions to begin with an introduction. Robin Hood had written her a statement to read. She would then tell her story, followed by the others. A question and answer session would be conducted afterwards.

At exactly noon, Natasha stood and approached the podium. She looked like an old pro. One would never have guessed she wasn't a seasoned press relations agent. She stood tall, scanning the audience from right to left. She made eye contact with many of the press members and began to read the prepared statement at noon. "I will begin by reading a prepared statement from Robin Hood M.D.."

The Southeastern representative for the New York Times looked at her watch and sighed. She wondered if this was some kind of a practical joke. She didn't have time for a 'prank' press conference.

*"Standing before you are three victims of crimes committed by health insurance companies. These crimes were thankfully halted while they were still in progress. I, Robin Hood M.D., using harsh measures, stopped the crimes. The criminals who perpetrated these crimes walk the streets free men, only because I allowed them to live."*

Suddenly, Natasha had everyone's full attention.

*"Health insurance companies feel they are omnipotent. They are correct. In fact, they are right on the money, no pun intended. Health insurance companies control the health care industry! They decide which treatments, medications, and diseases will be covered. Patients are held hostage on a daily basis by health insurance companies."*

Natasha took a drink of water after finishing the introduction. "This is my story...."

Timothy and Debra both addressed the audience after Natasha had finished. The reporters were spellbound.

Debra concluded, "now, we'll take a few questions from the media."

"Jim Hyatt, New York Times. Who is Robin Hood M.D.? Have any of you met this individual?"

The three looked at each other for a moment. Natasha rose and responded. "We only know he's our hero. None of us have met Robin Hood. Are there any other questions?"

"Ani Newton, Boston Globe. So none of you have met him, but do you have any idea what this Robin Hood looks like? You must know something. Do you think its one person or a group of people? Maybe a doctors' organization?" a petite woman with sparkling eyes asked.

"We're just thankful that Robin Hood has helped us, whoever, or whatever the entity is." Natasha turned and looked at Timothy and Debra for final confirmation. "I only hope that we can focus, not on who Robin Hood is, but on what we need to do as a society to take our health out of the hands of this corrupt heath insurance industry." She glanced at Timothy and Debra again, who nodded in agreement. "Next question?"

"Samantha Huet, AJC, can you each give me the names of your insurance companies please?"

Natasha jumped up first, "D.J.S. insurance company."

Timothy rose and leaned into the podium, "Henkins Commerce insurance company."

Debra could barely wait her turn, almost knocking Timothy over as she charged for the microphone. "Fulton Christian Hall insurance company."

The press conference lasted another 30 minutes. Samantha and Nate left early to file the story immediately and begin to attempt interviews with the CEOs of the three insurance companies. When she called in the story to her editor, he seemed very pleased.

Samantha dialed her assistant as she pulled out of the Biltmore parking lot. "I need the home and business addresses of the CEOs of the three insurance companies."

\* \* \*

"Mr. Bexley!" Samantha called to the CEO of Henkins Commerce Insurance Company.

Shocked at the presence of a stranger running towards him in his front yard, Theodore turned toward the approaching reporter. "Yes, may I help you?"

"I'm Samantha Huet of the Atlanta Journal and Constitution. I have a few questions for you."

"In my front yard?"

"It'll only take a few minutes, I promise!" Samantha flashed him her most vibrant smile, the one she'd never seen a prospective interviewee refuse. 'You gotta use what works!' her grandmother always told her. 'Nothing is beneath you if it accomplishes what you need to get done.' She chose not to think of herself as manipulative…she was just making sure God's gift of a perfect set of pearly whites didn't go to waste…

"Let's go inside," the CEO relented, hiding his annoyance as he wondered how the hell she got past security to get onto his property.

Theodore guided Samantha inside and called to his wife, "Honey, I have a guest. We're going to the library. Have the Katie bring us a couple glasses of sweet tea." They walked down a grand hallway with chandeliers and oil paintings in gilded gold frames that looked as if they could have been original Renoirs or Monet's. "Is that okay with you, Samantha?"

"Sure, that's fine," she acquiesced, trying not to allow herself to be impressed by the luxurious surroundings.

Theodore did not know what this was about, and he certainly did not intend to be investigated any further while exposed in his front yard. Even though his house was gated, and he had security employed 24/7, he was sure that even the grass had ears. He needed to gain some control of the situation before this young lady opened her mouth. He was an expert negotiator and knew that bringing her into his environment would soften her opening volley. Theodore showed her around his 3,000 square foot library. He showed off his extensive art collection. He particularly loved Monet and other Impressionist artists. He expounded on his benefactor status at the local museum as they finished their drinks.

"Have a seat," Theodore offered a seat on his couch, as he pulled up a chair. "Now, you said you have a few questions for me."

Samantha was in such awe that she had lost her fervor for the story. "Oh, yes, I wanted to ask you about a situation, I mean a kidnapping."

"I must say, I don't think I've kidnapped anyone lately," he winked flirtatiously.

"What I mean is, have you been kidnapped?"

"Ha, ha, ha," Theodore laughed. "Not that I am aware of."

Samantha felt like a damn idiot. What if the press conference had been a hoax?

"Mr. Bexley, a press conference was held today. A client of yours claims that you changed a ruling about a healthcare claim only because you were kidnapped and your life was threatened."

Theodore was trying with all of his might to remain composed. "My new friend, I think someone is pulling your leg. I would probably have called the police or the FBI if I had been kidnapped. Wouldn't you?"

Samantha was embarrassed. She stood, ignoring the rhetorical question. "I appreciate your time, Mr. Bexley."

Theodore walked Samantha to the door and bid her a proper farewell.

He closed the door behind her and walked into the bathroom. "Holy shit!" he murmured into the mirror. He hoped he had pulled off the charade. From the reporter's demeanor and quick departure, he felt like he had.

"I interviewed the CEO of Henkins Commerce Insurance Company," Samantha reported to the editor. "I think this may have been a hoax. He denied any kidnapping. In fact, he laughed at the very idea."

"Hmmmph!" the editor grumbled, momentarily absorbed in his peanut butter sandwich.

"He was very credible. To be honest, I felt stupid as heck as soon as it was obvious he had no idea about any kidnapping. He asked me wouldn't I call the police if I were kidnapped? I gracefully bowed out at that point."

The editor looked up from his sandwich and curtly concluded, "we'll talk about it tomorrow."

\*   \*   \*

First thing the next morning, John Bartol called Samantha into his office. She sauntered into his office slowly and deliberately, fearing that she was in trouble.

The editor began, "It seems that other media have gotten the same answers from the other two CEOs. I spoke with a friend at CNN who thinks this was all a hoax. None of the three CEOs claim to have to have been kidnapped. In fact, a PR firm has been hired by the three insurance companies to hold a press conference. It'll be tomorrow at the Commerce Club. I'll hold the story until we know all the facts. Once we have a better grasp on what actually happened, we can run the story in its entirety. Why don't you go back and interview the three patients individually. See if you can dig up any interesting facts about the circumstances leading up to the press conference. Then we can sit back and wait for one of our competitors to run a half-witted story. We'll be able to take full credit for a true story which tells what this is really about."

Samantha dragged her feet as she walked out of the editor's office. John watched her leave and smiled, making sure she didn't see him. He remembered many a time when he thought he had Watergate II in his hands, only to learn that the facts of the story did not pan out. She was a rookie and would learn, too. *That was one hell of a hoax*, he thought, shaking his head. *They had me going too, I have to admit.*

Samantha sat at her desk and sighed. She wanted a big story so badly she could taste it. She looked through her files and found the press release. Timothy Sims, Natasha Kapinski, and Debra Justin were the names of the patients. She thought, *if nothing else, this will make a good human interest story.* She decided to call her grandmother, a retired reporter, and ask her advice on how to proceed.

Grandma Huet answered the phone on the third ring. Samantha was pleased to hear her grandmother's sweet voice. Celia Huet had been a reporter with the AJC back in the days when women did not have jobs outside the home. Women certainly did not graduate from the University of Georgia journalism program with honors, work as a reporter, and later become a columnist with a prestigious newspaper in her era. Grandma Huet was a ground breaker. Samantha admired her feisty grandmother. She wanted to be as strong as her.

"Grandma, can I get some advice?"

"Man problems? Honey, I told you about men."

"No, Grandma," Samantha giggled, knowing full well that her grandma was just pulling her leg. "It's a journalist issue."

"Well, I might be able to help with that one too."

Samantha explained the situation to Celia in great detail.

"Why did you go into the CEO's house? Why didn't you ask your questions in his yard?"

"I just followed him into the house without really thinking about it when he invited me in. I was just happy he agreed to be interviewed. He showed me his library and his art collection."

"Were you there to see his art or to find out the facts?"

"I see your point. But I was glad I wasn't too pushy once I realized it was obvious that he hadn't been kidnapped. I guess the whole thing was just a hoax."

"The result was acceptable, but you have to be more assertive. You have to take charge of the interview. If you can't get the answers any other way, then you may have to follow along for a while. The key is to remember what your job is."

"What about the three patients. How should I handle this?"

"Find out how they each learned about this Robin Hood character. How did each patient know each other? How were they invited to the press conference? Do they think this is a hoax? Was there really any evidence that the insurance company had a drastic change of heart? If so, why did they change their minds? Did they correspond with Robin Hood? That'll be a good start for you. Just get them talking."

"Yeah, I guess that'll work. Thanks, Grandma."

# CHAPTER ELEVEN

"Welcome to the Commerce Club's weekly luncheon. Today we have a feature speaker. Amy Nater will discuss the recent claims of kidnappings of the CEOs of some of the major health insurance companies. She'll take questions after her statement," began the moderator of the Atlanta Press Club's weekly gathering.

Amy Nater approached the podium as the applause reached a crescendo. "Rumors and hoaxes are ancient means to an end. That end is attention. People with no singing ability whatsoever, will audition for a show like *American Idol.* Why do they do that? For attention! Kidnapping the CEOs of insurance companies and torturing them would certainly get the media's attention. When I heard the story, it got my attention. I hate to tell you guys, but Theodore Bexley Jr., Jimbo Simmons, and Jonathan Willingham were not kidnapped and tortured. Robin Hood M.D.? Come on, guys! I know for a fact that the AJC and CNN reporters have had flat-out denials from the CEOs about these ridiculous allegations. And I mean, really, who are we going to believe —important heads of industry or some anonymous freak who won't even show his face in public? I hope these statements are in print soon."

Samantha was sitting in the front row and nearly choked on her $30 salad as the speaker peered in her direction.

"The initial story ran by the Washington Tribune is incomplete and uncorroborated. As far as I can tell, this is the only news agency that has put this nonsense in print so far. I hope the press in the room will continue to look for the missing facts in this strange situation before they print any more damaging and ridiculous stories about these CEOs and their companies. I'll be happy to take any questions now."

"Please go to the microphone located in the center of the room if you have questions," the moderator instructed.

A mad rush of reporters made their way to the microphone.

"Jim Griff, New York Times. Why did the insurance companies suddenly change their rulings regarding the three patients? It certainly seems that they were forced to take another direction in each of the three cases."

Amy Nater replied; "It was made to seem that way by the people who perpetuated this hoax. In fact, if you look carefully at each of the three cases, you'll see that they were under medical review. The cases were to be certified for payment at some point. This was a dramatic turn of events for the family."

"Samantha Huet, Atlanta Journal and Constitution. You claim this was all a hoax. Who do you claim is involved in the hoax?"

"This Robin Hood M.D. character is the most obvious spin-master in this story —probably some angry anti-insurance activist, or a group of them. I'm not sure what role the three patients play in this, if any. Their speeches were likely scripted for them by the pranksters at the bottom of this whole joke. If you'll remember, the patient named Natasha even read a script clearly stated as the words of Robin Hood before she began her story. I suspect that the three patients were pawns in the hoax and not perpetrators."

"Amy Hurt, Los Angeles Times. In the age of rising health costs and diminished insurance coverage, what message do you think Robin Hood is trying to convey with this hoax?"

The press relations agent laughed at the question. "I'd like to ask the question to Robin Hood M.D. personally. I certainly can't answer this one for him."

"Follow up, please. Do you think we need health insurance reform? Do you feel that Robin Hood M.D. is really trying to encourage reform?"

"The health insurance industry is one of the most heavily monitored and regulated industries in this country. If they were more regulated they wouldn't survive. Increasing government interference in corporations is un-American. Do you want a government-run insurance agency? Just think about that scenario for a moment," retorted Amy as she looked piercingly into the network camera.

*   *   *

Natasha and Samantha meet in a conference room at Natasha's University.

"Natasha, how did you learn about Robin Hood M.D.?" began Samantha.

"I really would rather not talk about that, it's somewhat of a private matter."

"Okay, we can come back to that later. Did you know Timothy and Debra before the press conference?"

"No, that was the first time we met."

"How were you invited to the press conference?"

"I received a letter in the mail from Robin Hood M.D.. It was addressed to all three of us."

"May I see the letter please?"

Natasha thought for a few moments. She was thankful to this person for her life and she didn't want to get him in trouble. It appeared that the press thought this was all a hoax. In any other circumstance, Natasha could care less about what the media thought, but she knew that what she said or did not say could be damaging to whoever or whatever had saved her. She hated to be in this bind. She felt like it was a damned if she did, damned if she didn't situation. Anything she revealed might be used against Robin Hood, but if she concealed the truth they'd go on thinking it was all a hoax.

Natasha finally looked up to level Samantha square in the eyes and decided it was better to keep anything she knew to herself for the moment. "I think I may have thrown that away."

*Bullshit*, Samantha thought to herself. She opted for a more appropriate response, "Hmm. That certainly is a shame."

"I guess I should have saved it, huh?"

Samantha searched Natasha's face and watched her body language as she had been taught in journalism school. Natasha had crossed her arms and legs and gazed downwards at her shoes. She was hiding something and she was obviously lying about the letter.

"Do you think this is a hoax? And if so, are you involved in it?"

Natasha's posture changed at the now abrasive tone of the reporter. "I beg your pardon? I nearly died because of that insurance company's greed. I thought of shooting myself to stop the headaches."

Samantha opted to stay in control of the interview. She held out her right hand palm out, signaling Natasha to stop. "I didn't mean to upset you. I'm not insinuating that you haven't suffered. I, and the country, need to know the truth. Was this a hoax?"

Natasha had tears in her eyes and her face was red. "As I was saying, at the point that I was ready to die, the insurance company suddenly had a change of heart and allowed payment for the study. You heard my story at the press conference, did you not?"

"Yes ma'am, I heard your story."

Natasha sure as hell was not going to tell this reporter that her mother had e-mailed Robin Hood M.D.. This may get him caught and her mother in trouble. "After I recovered from the surgery, I received the letter from Robin Hood M.D. asking the three of us to hold a press conference. That is how I learned about the kidnappings. To answer the question, I don't know of any hoax, and frankly do not care what it was. I am alive because something happened to make the insurance company change its mind!"

"Why do you think the decision makers at the insurance company changed their minds about payment for the study at the last minute?"

"I don't know. Dr. Harrison said they always do things like this so they can save money."

"Did you personally have any correspondence with Robin Hood M.D.?"

"No."

"Did any of your family or friends talk to or contact Robin Hood M.D.?"

"No," Natasha lied.

"Are you Robin Hood M.D.?"

Natasha thought for a second before she answered. "What do you think, Lois Lane? --that I faked my near comatose state, hurdled out of my hospital bed, and kidnapped a few CEOs so I could save the day?"

Samantha reached out and touched the young lady on the arm and replied, "I don't know, darling. You look like a superwoman to me." Samantha wanted to lighten up the interview with a few stupid questions, and befriend her, as her grandmother had suggested... Anything to get her talking again.

"You handle yourself very well in front of cameras. Do you want to be a public figure?"

"I'm a graduate student."

"What's your major?"

"Foreign affairs. Actually, International Studies. I will likely end up doing some kind of PR work."

"You're well suited for it. I was very impressed the other day." Samantha had a few more tough questions. She hoped her outright flattery wouldn't be construed as insincere. Though Sam's every word was measured as she plotted to get her story, she honestly did have a great sense of admiration for the serious young grad student.

"Thank you."

"Natasha, I need to ask you about a delicate situation. It's my job and I have to ask you. Is that okay?"

"Depends on what the questions are," asserted Natasha.

"It is public record that your mother was arrested for assault at your insurance company. It seems that the company's legal department has spoken with the District Attorney's office and the plan is to not pursue criminal charges. Apparently, she was upset with the company for not allowing you to have an X-ray done. Of course, this was resolved. Can we talk about this?"

"Sorry, I'm not going to comment on that, Samantha."

"May I ask why not?"

"It's a private matter. My mother is a very dignified lady. She felt enormous pressure to do something. The insurance company would not talk to her, she thought that I was going to die, and she went to the company for answers. When she ran into the smart ass receptionist who had hung up on her, she lost it. Put yourself in her position." Natasha realized she had said too much, as she watched the steady rotation of the reel in the small recorder.

Samantha gestured in a fluster with her finger as she pondered her next questions. "I'm having trouble understanding here. Did your mother have some sort of contact with Robin Hood M.D.? If she was mad as hell and scared on top of it, wouldn't she have contacted just about anyone in order to help her daughter? Did someone put her in contact with this person? Is she responsible for this hoax? Is there even a real Robin Hood M.D., or did you two cook this up to get back at the insurance company?"

With a controlled smirk, Natasha shushed the flustered reporter. "You have a lot of questions, and I'm all out of answers." Natasha stood and walked out of the room.

"Well Grandma, I guess I screwed that one up too," Samantha sighed into the empty room.

\*    \*    \*

Samantha had better luck with Timothy and Debra. Both gave her copies of the letter from Robin Hood M.D.. The two had more credible denials of any relationship with the kidnapper. They were believable. But it continued to bother her that she couldn't figure out what Natasha and her mother were trying to hide and why!

Samantha reported her progress on the story to the editor. She sat down at her desk and looked at the picture of her dog. She checked her e-mail. She gasped as she looked at the list of incoming mail. One of them was addressed from ROBIN HOOD M.D.. She opened the mail, looking around to make sure she was alone.

MS. HUET, I WISH TO CLEAR UP A FEW THINGS. I EXPECT YOU WILL WANT TO SHARE THIS WITH THE WORLD IN YOUR NEWS STORY. HOAX? CLICK ON THE VIDEO ATTACHMENT AND SEE FOR YOURSELF!

Samantha again glanced over her shoulder to see if anyone was looking. She clicked on the attached icon and stared at the video display window. Scanning the news office again to see if she had any spectators, she clicked on the 'play' tab.

Sound blared across the room. She had not realized that her speaker volume was wide open. She quickly reduced the volume and began to watch the video labeled 'Jimbo Simmons.' She gasped, her hand fluttering at her mouth as she realized what she was seeing.

Jimbo Simmons sat in front of an American flag reading a statement. A banner hung just above the flag reading, AMERICANS HELD HOSTAGE. The CEO looked disheveled and very worried. Samantha had seen an interview with the CEO previously. He usually had a commanding presence in front of the camera. In the video he looked pale and fearful. A masked man appeared in the corner of the screen. He appeared to have a gun in his hand.

She watched all three videos, each labeled with the name of each captive CEO. All three insurance executives read the same incriminating statement. When the last of the videos ended, ten minutes slipped by before the phone in the next cubicle rang breaking the spell and startling her out of her daydreams. This was the kind of journalism she had dreamed of as a small child. It was her fierce desire to aspire to this kind of news coverage that had kept her at it, despite all the disappointing leads and dead end interviews she'd pursued. Finally she had the 'big story.' *This was a son of a bitch, too* she thought as she headed for the editor's office. She moved slowly, savoring the delicious secret that was as of yet hers alone to share with the world. She was so excited she felt she could almost explode at the seams! Grandma was going to love this!

\* \* \*

John Bartol sat at Samantha's desk as he was asked to do. "This had better be good," he grumbled. Samantha opened her email inbox and showed her boss the message from Robin Hood M.D.. He read it in silence. Samantha studied him for any kind of a response as he read, but his years of experience had seasoned his poker face. He made no outward display of emotion other than slightly raising his right brow. He turned to look at her when he was finished reading. She clicked play on the computer and the three videos began. He watched in disbelief. "What in the hell is this?" the normally dignified editor uttered. He turned to stare at her as the third video ended. "So, it seems that the three were kidnapped after all! Why in the hell would someone deny being kidnapped?"

"That's exactly what I'm going to find out!" Samantha responded in a sudden burst of anger as she realized: "That son of a bitch lied to me!"

"Samantha, I believe you may just have that big story you've been after. Before you do anything else, write this up and have it on my desk ASAP. I hope he hasn't sent this e-mail to anyone else. This would be an incredible exclusive for us! If we play our cards right, you can interview the CEOs, show them the videos, and get their response. All the other media will still be trying to scramble for the CEO interviews and not be getting anywhere. They'll be running 'hoax' stories and we'll be a mile ahead of them."

John abruptly jumped from his seat and jostled back towards his office. He turned and looked at Samantha. "Get to work!" he commanded.

Samantha knew she was going to spend the night at the office. She called a Chinese restaurant and placed her 'to go' order. She cancelled her date for later in the evening and made a quick call to her grandmother. She pulled out all of her files on the case and began to write.

She was surprised that she had completed the report by midnight. She looked at the headline and smiled to herself. She placed it on the editor's desk and made her way to her car. She was going to wake up Mr. Bexley's ass in the morning. She hoped she could interview the other CEOs before the story was broken, but realized the logistics were not in her favor as the other two would require air travel.

# CHAPTER TWELVE

"Run it! Run the damn article! This looks great!" John Bartol shouted at the top of his lungs to anyone in ear shot. "Where's Samantha?" he boomed.

"I haven't seen her this morning," the reporter in the adjacent cubicle to Samantha's answered.

"I want this on the front page!" John demanded to the chief.

"Let me see what you're so excited about?" The editor in chief read for a moment and then looked at John quizzically. He read on and walked towards his computer. "I want to see the videos she's referencing in the article." He pulled up the email and watched the videos. He looked up at John and smiled. "Samantha will be getting her own office if she keeps this up! Front page tomorrow. Let's get it done!"

\* \* \*

The door bell echoed throughout the house. "What in the hell is that?" Theodore sat up and looked at his clock. It read 4:45 am. The door bell chimed again, confirming the intrusion to his sleep. "Who in the hell is at the door this time of the morning?" Theodore asked his wife. She stretched an arm without opening her eyes and rolled over, mumbling into her pillow, "maybe the postman," before rolling over and snoring again. He climbed out of bed, pulled on his robe, and stumbled towards the door.

Theodore opened the door and found Samantha with a scowl on her face. She began, offering no apology or explanation with her cross examination. "You lied to me! We are going to get some things straight!"

"Ms. Samantha, it is four in the morning, what could be that important! Why don't you come inside?"

"No, I will stay right here. I want to show you what's so important!" She pulled a laptop from her bag and played the video. "I want you to explain this."

His composure changed as he watched himself read the statement on the screen. Samantha was silent, watching his face for a reaction. He certainly had one. In fact he had several varied reactions. His faced turned red, then pale. He slumped against the door. Beads of sweat formed on his forehead. The video finished without a word from the now shaken CEO.

"It seems that you were kidnapped, Mr. Bexley. Why did you lie about this earlier?"

The CEO shook his head, in shock and unable to find his voice.

Samantha continued her barrage of questions. "You were embarrassed about your company's behavior in the Sims case, so you couldn't say it took a kidnapping to save the boy's life, could you?"

Theodore pulled himself inside the door and whispered hoarsely, "No comment." He closed the door slowly in Samantha's face.

"Who was at the door?" Mrs. Bexley mumbled as Theodore came back into the bedroom.

"A reporter."

"At this hour?"

"I'll tell you later." He tottered into the bathroom, hoping that a swallow of cold water would dislodge the lump in his throat.

\* \* \*

"Samantha, great job! Front page news! You have the headline story, young lady," the editor congratulated the reporter.

"Thanks. I gave Mr. Bexley a wake-up call. He is not a happy camper."

"What did he say?"

"What could he say? He was speechless. Can you get me to the other two CEOs?"

"I'll call in tickets for you to pick up at the Delta counter at Hartsfield-Jackson Airport. The story runs in 24 hours. You'll need to hurry. We can run the story of the CEO's reaction in the evening edition tomorrow if you e-mail me the story."

"Consider it done."

"You've done one heck of a job on this story. I'm proud of you."

Samantha was honored. Compliments were rare from her boss. "Thank you," she replied humbly. She still couldn't believe her luck. This was just too good to be true!

"NOT A HOAX!" the headline ran.

VIDEO EVIDENCE PROVES THAT ROBIN HOOD M.D. KIDNAPS THREE CEOs OF HEALTH INSURANCE COMPANIES, FORCING LIFE-SAVING PROCEDURES TO BE COVERED.

Samantha's story, as expected by the paper's editors, sparked a flurry of related news stories. At one of her stopovers, as Samantha was waiting to transfer planes, she was pleased to see that CNN was all over it. All the passengers waiting at the gate around her were glued to the T.V. suspended from the ceiling. As "breaking news" flashed across the screen, Samantha watched along with everyone else and swelled with pride. It was all she could do to keep from jumping up, taking a bow and announcing, "Hey everyone, this is my story!" but she remained calm and collected, silently basking in the glory.

"Welcome to CNN Headline News with Bob Thomas. We have a breaking story. The Atlanta Journal Constitution reports in its headlines that the kidnappings of CEOs of three major Atlanta-based health insurance companies did, in fact, occur. Apparently we have video evidence that was produced by, of all people, the kidnapper. Let's look at the videos."

Bob Thomas came on and Samantha caught her breath as it sank in. *Her* story coming out of the mouth of *Bob Thomas!* "You are entering a no spin zone," he announced in that unmistakable "breaking news" tone of voice, which was a mix of detached indifference and boundless excitement. "Breaking news today from the Atlanta Journal Constitution that the alleged kidnappings of three health insurance CEOs is not a hoax. Video evidence has surfaced that confirms the three

Chief Executive Officers were in fact kidnapped. Let's watch the videos, and then we'll come back and discuss the facts with an advocate and an opponent of the state of things in the health insurance industry. The CEOs and their public relations company have all denied comment."

"Let's start with Dr. Tom Sercy, a vocal opponent of the health insurance industry. What say you about the videos?"

Dr. Sercy leaned into his microphone with an air of authority. "I think it's about time we had a hero step up and punish the leaders of this corrupt industry. It is going to take drastic action in order to get the attention of congress."

"Wait a minute," the industry advocate Hugh Turner interrupted, "you're out of line! If the CEOs were kidnapped and held against their will, it's nothing to celebrate."

"Let me finish," Tom continued. "Patients suffer daily at the hands of these millionaires. I hope they suffered! They make millions of dollars by holding patients hostage. The banner above their heads read 'America Held Hostage.' That says it all."

"Why do you hate the health insurance industry so much?" Bob Thomas asked, hoping to invoke an inflammatory response.

"In a word, greed. They steal health from patients."

"Come on," complained Mr. Turner: "any industry has its downsides. The great majority of people are perfectly happy with their health insurance plan. Companies purchase the plans for employees. The plans vary in what's covered. The most common dispute with insurance companies is over uncovered services. The only reason any service is not covered is because the client doesn't purchase it. That's not the fault of the insurance companies."

"Nothing is the insurance companies' fault, is it?" Dr. Sercy snorted. "According to you guys, they're just an innocent business doing all good and no harm."

The host interrupted, "Okay, give us an example of just one time where they have actually done harm to a patient."

"Just one?" asked Mr. Sercy.

"Just one," clarified the host.

"In order to make a larger profit, the insurance companies require that drugs prescribed by a doctor be on a formulary. The insurance companies all have their own formularies. They negotiate the cheapest price with the drug companies, thus setting the formularies. There are some drugs that patients need that aren't on the formularies. For example, a young girl in my hometown was on a strong anti-psychotic drug, and had been well controlled on this medication for years. Her insurance coverage changed and the company refused to pay for the medication. Before the company would even reconsider paying for the more expensive medication, they insisted she try a drug that she had already tried and found ineffective. She ended up having to be put in a psychiatric hospital on multiple occasions. She attempted suicide once."

"The State of Georgia is not taking new enrollments for its program for children from low income families because of financial constraints," responded Mr. Turner. "They don't have enough money to operate. Do you think that not having a formulary would help the situation?"

"I think that the CEO should take a pay cut before children are denied their medications. However, you know this is not going to happen," Dr. Sercy retorted sarcastically. "The CEOs are the first to profit and the last to lose. When a company fails, guess what? They bail out with their golden parachutes. The CEO's always win!

"They're just doing their job, no different than any other heads of industry." Mr. Turner insisted.

"No different, except that every decision they make puts people's lives at stake." grumbled Dr. Sercy.

"So, Mr. Turner, if the CEO's aren't at fault they have nothing to hide. Are we going to be able to talk with them any time soon?" the host asked.

"They're not available for comment at this time," Mr. Turner conceded.

"Well, we're just about out of time. I'll give you the last word, Mr. Turner," the host concluded.

"Much maligned, the health insurance industry is who 'pays the fiddler' in this country. We pay the bills. We are overregulated, but that's not enough for the liberals. Overpaid doctors order unnecessary tests and expensive drugs when an inexpensive generic would work just as well, and we're supposed to look the other way, wasting our clients' money."

"Okay, well, thanks to both of you. You obviously are not going to come to common ground on your feelings about insurance companies. We'll be back tomorrow with an exclusive interview with a patient who claims to be second cousins with Robin Hood M.D.. Back to you, Jim."

Amy Nater watched the news from home. She shook her head and impatiently scanned the other channels, stopping at the NBC news.

"We have on the show today criminal psychologist Brent Jude. Sir, I understand you've viewed the videos. Is it your opinion that they're real?"

"Yes. I think that the three men shown are the CEOs in question. It appears that each of them is under great stress. Mr. Simmons especially, looks in extremis. I see no evidence of tampering or editing of the videos. These are low tech videos as one would expect when making a home video. The kidnapper likely had a hidden camera. The CEO's were not looking in the direction of the camera while they were reading."

The MSNBC reporter turned to the camera and reiterated: "it appears that the videos are authentic, folks."

Amy sighed and reached for the remote again. "Shit!" she grumbled as she continued to skim channels. It was worse than she thought. This thing was already plastered on every channel. She got up in disgust, and went to the kitchen for more coffee.

From the kitchen, she could hear that Meet the Press was about to begin and she rushed back to the living room.

The moderator began: "Do we need health insurance reform? This is the topic on today's Meet the Press. The panel today is Democratic Senator Jay Treadwell, Republican Representative Daniel Richter, Natasha Kapinski, a patient who claims she would have died because of insurance company greed, but for the heroics of a modern day Robin Hood, and Atlanta Journal Constitution reporter Samantha Huet. Notably absent today are the three CEOs who were reportedly kidnapped and tortured by Robin Hood M.D.. They were invited on the show but declined to participate."

Amy Nater turned down the volume and reached for her cell phone to call her office. "I want to arrange a meeting at our island retreat. Call Jimbo, Jonathan, and Theodore and make arrangements to get their asses there so we can sort this mess out. Also, I want to talk to Samantha Huett at the AJC today. We have a snowball sitting at the top of a hill and it's about to start rolling." She turned the volume up just as the moderator was opening the discussion with a question to Ms. Huet.

"Samantha, you broke this bizarre story to the world. How did you learn about this story?"

"I received a press release, as many reporters did, inviting the press to a press conference which broke the story. I was later contacted by an anonymous source leading me to the videos."

"It seems that you were way ahead of the other media. You must have had access to an insider," the host inquired.

"I'm not denying that fact," Samantha testified. She allowed herself a small grin.

The host continued: "I surmise that we're not going to learn the identity of the source of your information."

Samantha had never been interviewed. She certainly had never been asked to be a panelist on a national talk show. She was trying to watch her body language and posture, hoping she'd come across as composed and professional. The questions, however, were irritating and unprofessional. Did this asshole think she was going to expose her source on national television? He was obviously playing with the fact that she was an unseasoned reporter.

Samantha answered: "you surmise correctly. My source has my confidence."

The host changed the subject. "Senator Treadwell, do you think that the health insurance industry needs further regulation?"

"I feel that they are properly regulated. They are monitored at both the State and Federal level. The health insurance industry is one of the most heavily monitored entities in the country."

Representative Richter interjected: "I feel much more can be done. I have many constituents who are very unhappy with their health insurance companies. They've had some serious issues with their coverage, and let me tell you, I've heard some horror stories from these folks. Insurance companies are refusing to pay for tests, procedures, and prescription drugs."

Natasha jumped in: "I would have been dead if Robin Hood M.D. had not intervened on my behalf. I had an aneurysm that was about to rupture, and the insurance company would not pay for me to have the proper testing needed to find the problem. I had to have emergency surgery, which saved my life, after Robin Hood forced the study to be done."

The moderator nodded gravely and remarked: "We now have video evidence to prove that in several cases, the insurance companies were forced by violence to change their rulings. Natasha has given us dramatic evidence of what she endured at the hands of her insurance company in the initial press conference. You really suffered, did you not?"

"I suffered beyond belief. I am so blessed that someone stepped in and stopped my suffering." Tears filled Natasha's eyes as she spoke. "I was in terrible pain. I had a savior. I'm here today to speak up for those who do not. I was lucky. What about all of the others who have to deal with these companies without any help? It's David versus Goliath!" Natasha made eye contact with each of the congressmen. "We need your help." She raised her voice. "Please help the American people. We don't have the clout to fight these companies by ourselves."

The congressmen were caught off guard. They were both accustomed to dealing with pundits and politicians in this setting. They had to be careful about what was said to this young lady, as she was truly a citizen who had been victimized.

The host pushed the issue along. "Would congress consider holding hearings to ensure that the health insurance companies are treating patients fairly? Senator Treadwell and Representative Richter, what do you say?"

The senator began, "I'd be happy to look into this matter. As I was implying earlier, there are means already in place to review cases in question. That being said, I think that if the citizens of this country feel that the process is not working, then congress is compelled to hear the complaints."

"It's a rare occasion when this happens, but today I agree with the senator," the representative agreed. "I'm normally a conservative, who unlike many of my colleagues, is not a fan of the health insurance industry; and the senator is on the left on most issues, but this one crosses the boundaries of the great political divide. We need to protect the citizens of the United States."

The show ended without Samantha getting to say another word. She walked off the set and found her bag. Her cell phone had two messages. The first was from her grandmother. The second was an unfamiliar number. She listened to the message in disbelief. It was from Robin Hood M.D.. He asked her to meet him at the Fulton County Police Department at 8 p.m. He planned to turn himself in. Samantha's heart skipped a beat. She looked around for a chair, suddenly feeling faint.

# CHAPTER THIRTEEN

The house sat 500 yards off the beach. Though it was several stories high, it covered so much square footage that it appeared low-lying, blending in with the natural terrain. Anyone passing from a distance by boat who didn't know it was there would certainly mistake it as a continuation of the level cliffs and dunes that scattered over this stretch of coast. The siding of the house was sand-colored, owing to the bricks made from the most expensive Egyptian clay money could buy. The black shutters on every window were hand-carved out of ivory and bordered with patterns of semi-precious stones. If you looked out the east windows on the ground level, only trees were visible, which buffered the house from the beach. This was where all of the business dealings were done. A multi-level screened-in porch encompassed the entire eastern side of the house. It was lined with rocking chairs, hammocks, and bench swings, all facing the ocean. The pool house, set off behind the tennis courts and surrounded with exquisite grottos, gardens, and fountains, was large enough to throw a banquet for 150 people. The pool was a mosaic of imported Italian marble of different shades, which, when viewed from the highest diving board, had the appearance of a sun setting over a mountainous horizon. The guest house was larger than the average home, and was set off in its own grove of palms beyond the pool.

Each CEO had his own private wing in the upper level of the house complete with kitchen suites, jacuzzi baths, walk-in closets, and personal attendants to cater to their every whim. They had all arrived at the airport at different times, and had been shuttled to the house. The island airport was lined with leer jets and limousines. Amy Nater was bunking in the guest house. One of her assistants was monitoring the media reports.

Amy was particularly disgruntled after having spoken to Samantha Huet at the AJC. She had gotten nowhere with the young reporter. She had asked to speak to Ms. Huet off the record, and she was told that she would need to get permission from her editors before she engaged in 'off the record' activities.

A meeting was scheduled that evening after dinner. A scheduling board was placed in each of the private wings. The CEOs were encouraged to go to the beach and unwind. Activities could be arranged if anyone wished to participate. Jonathan and Jimbo decided to go horseback riding. Theodore decided to sip a cocktail and read a mindless mystery novel on the back porch. They all met back at the beach house dining room for a dinner of caper roasted quail on a bed of saffron quinoa with an infusion of summer beets and portabella mushrooms. The meal was fine, but the conversation was lacking, as everyone knew an intense meeting was about to begin. Despite their best efforts, no one had relaxed that day. Jimbo's horse, sensing his tension, had spooked when a bird swooped up from the underbrush, rearing up and nearly throwing Jimbo from the saddle. Jonathan had forgotten to discard the riding pants he'd sworn never to wear again after his last horse ride, and had itched and chafed in them all afternoon. And Theodore was just too distracted to focus on reading, and too uptight to nap, even after his third cocktail. The alcohol didn't give him a pleasant buzz. He just ended up with a pounding headache.

The meeting began as dessert was served. Amy opened the meeting. "To say we have a public relations dilemma would be like saying the Titanic had a slight moisture problem. When you have a mess like this, you have to sit down, catch your breath, and regroup. We are here to collectively take a deep breath and have a brief window of escape from the media."

Amy paused a moment, took an exaggerated deep breath, and continued, "We have a kidnapper vying for attention, and victims of kidnappings running for cover. Odd things float to the top of the media's creamy minds very quickly. I hope I can help demystify this

mess for the media. Hopefully, we won't have any more surprises. I want to talk about what's going on in the news talk show circuit as we speak. But before that, I need some insight as to what happened to each of you. Jimbo, let's start with you please."

"I haven't talked to anyone about this," Jimbo began sheepishly, looking down at his half-devoured lemon pecan cheesecake. "I was kidnapped and nearly choked to death by a psychopath. I really thought I was a dead man. He threatened to kill my family if I told anyone about the incident. I didn't know he had videotaped the confession." He went on to describe the kidnapping in gory detail.

There was an awkward silence after he finished. Theodore picked at a hangnail, while Jonathan studied the grain in the hardwood floor beneath the table. Amy broke the silence. "Jonathan, how about you?" Jonathan heaved a deep sigh and reluctantly shared his story, Theodore following suit. All three CEOs described the same fear of getting the authorities involved. Amy had to shake herself back into action, as she contemplated the horror that her clients had endured.

"Okay. We're going to need to call in Congressional favors, and quickly. On Meet the Press, one of our biggest supporters, Senator Jay Treadwell agreed to a Congressional hearing looking into the practices of the healthcare industry. This is a guy who we own, or thought we owned. We have to put the brakes on this hearing business immediately. Tomorrow I want each of you to call all of the congressmen on the list in your packets. I've called your lobbyists and put a fire under their asses, reminding them how much money you've invested to "educate" Congress."

"How do we respond to the media?" Jonathan asked.

"The truth will set you free. We have to put forth some type of response. No comment looks and smells guilty. You all are victims. You are not guilty of anything. If you're kidnapped, you call the police. We're going to call the FBI and tell them the details of the kidnapping. When the media asks, we'll tell them that the authorities are involved, and we're unable to comment on an active investigation; however, when fearing for the life of your family you'll do anything to prevent their harm. This would include denying a kidnapping."

"How do we explain the sudden change in heart about the coverage for the cases?"

Amy tapped the ends of her cupped fingers together. "That, unfortunately, is going to be like putting wax on a junk yard car. Avoid the question. Spin the question. Defer the question. Whatever you do, do not answer this question!"

"What happened to 'the truth will set you free?'" asked Theodore.

"Well, you'll be only partially free, then." A much needed and welcomed burst of laughter erupted around the table. "The truth is on our side in a portion of this situation, but not in total. Guys, this is a damn tough spot you're in. I'm having to pull out all the stops for this one. You three are not going on national television and admitting to changing your rulings on these cases because you were forced to do so. Even if the force was a physical threat that any reasonable person would have yielded to, the perception will be that you changed because you knew you were wrong."

"Yeah, did you all see what the news channels were playing all day yesterday?" Jimbo began. "We are in for an uphill battle. It didn't take long for our enemies to come out of the woodworks. They've been waiting for any opportunity to jump all over something like this."

"We are going to have the same chances of coming out of this unscathed, as the fisherman in the 'Old Man and the Sea' had at getting his big fish to market," conceded Amy, hoping the three had read the classic. "We have to hope that we have at least a little fish left at the end of the day."

"This whole thing stinks like a dead sail fish," Theodore reminisced for a moment about Hemingway.

"Tomorrow we need a big push from you guys. The congressmen need to recall everything you've done for them: Trips, dinners, millions for campaigns and slush funds. It's payback time!" Amy barked. "We'll contact the FBI in the morning. I'm sure they've already become interested in these events. I'll send out a press release." She rose and pushed in her chair. "Now I suggest everyone get a good night's sleep. You'll need it."

*   *   *

"I wish to speak directly with Senator Treadwell," Theodore Bexley explained to the senator's aide.

"Just a moment, I'll see if I can locate Mr. Treadwell," the young female voice cooed cheerfully. A minute later she came back on the line. "I'm sorry. He's not available at this time, Mr. Bexley."

"Make him available!"

"I'm sorry. I have specific orders from the Senator that he's not to be disturbed. Would you like to speak to his—"

"You heard me, I want to speak with him and no one else!" Theodore interrupted, raising his voice authoritatively.

"Okay, I'll try again to get him on the phone with you."

"You try very hard. Tell him this is an emergency. I'll wait on the line."

It was a full 10 minutes before he was finally connected with the Senator. He was just about to give up waiting when Mr. Treadwell came on the line, breathing heavy from running to the phone. "Ted, I'm in an important session. Can I call you back?"

"I need you!"

"I know what this is about. I'll be glad to talk with you at a later time."

"I had my people take a look at our books. We've donated 4 million dollars to your campaign and much more over your term. Calling for a congressional hearing into my industry is not what I had in mind when I contributed those funds, Senator."

Senator Treadwell's posture inadvertently shifted from relaxed to defensive, as his jaw clinched and he changed the receiver from his right hand to his left. He held up an index finger and mouthed to the agitated aide to wait a minute, as she frantically gestured that the committee was waiting for him. She heaved an exasperated sigh and sped back to the hearing room to notify the participants of his delay. "For years I've posed as a Republican for your benefit." the Senator responded in his most practiced diplomatic tone. "On Meet the Press I stood firm ground for your industry until it became obvious to everyone that I was a paid spokesman for the health insurance industry. The conservative representatives called for a hearing. When the ball was hit to me, I could either acquiesce or become a paid pundit. I had to make a choice. If you haven't noticed, it is 'hot in the kitchen.' Now I'm sorry, but it may just get too hot for me to help you."

"This is when I need you, damn it! When the heat is on! Don't run away from me now, Senator." Theodore was now shouting: "You stand up and fight for us."

The Senator turned to look and see if anyone was looking, and lowered his voice. "Every time a bill came along that may have been the least bit injurious to you insurance people, I fought like a gladiator to stop it. I championed every pro-insurance bill. It is well known where I stand with the health insurance industry and your opponents, which are becoming many. That being said, I can't stand in front of a freight train all alone and take the blunt of the blow, while you guys hide behind your public relations firm and refuse to comment. How in the hell do you think the public will treat me if I stand alone, defying a massive public outcry, and fight for you? The bottom line is that the public is fed up with your bullshit."

"There is not a massive public outcry," the CEO countered.

"Read the papers, Theodore, watch the news, check the internet! A storm is brewing and the winds are coming. We're all going to have to take shelter and ride this hurricane out, my friend. As much as I would like to help you, I'll have to be very careful not to commit suicide in the process. I live or die by votes. I can't alienate my constituency to help you. Now, I'm sorry, but I really do have to go."

The dial tone roared as Theodore looked at the receiver in his hand. He had not feared the loss of his job until now. He was used to getting exactly what he wanted from Congress. He felt he was suddenly missing an arm or leg. He had just lost the most powerful ally that his industry had ever known. He laughed aloud at the absurd realization that sprung to mind. *In the end, 4 million dollars wasn't as valuable as a maniac kidnapper.* "Well shit!" he cursed aloud.

Theodore joined the other two CEOs and the public relations pro in the television room. "Did you two have any luck with your contacts in Congress?" Theodore inquired hopefully.

"No," Jonathan grumbled. "I've gotten that son of a bitch elected every year. I was his largest fund raiser last year. Now, he's unable to help me because the public pressure is too great."

"Ditto," Jimbo concurred.

Amy looked worried as she listened to the bad news. She turned her attention back to the news program, and watched the CEOs burn in effigy before her eyes. As the day passed, she was continually hanging between anxiety and tedium. Normally she was able to maintain enough of a professional distance to relax and enjoy her surroundings, whatever they were. This time was different. She barely even noticed the perfect weather, the soothing rhythmic sound of ocean waves, the bright colors of the lush gardens around the grounds of the beach house. She'd never had to deal with such a media disaster. She was beginning to concede, inwardly, that these three were dead meat. She wanted to keep her job, so she continued to rack her brain for a way to fight this mess. She gulped down her double espresso, wishing she didn't have to face the CEOs, who waited expectantly for her to come up with a solution to bale them out. "Guys, it looks like we are going to have to step back and allow the flames to burn out. I had hoped we could put the brakes on a congressional hearing, but it's looking more difficult than I thought it would be."

Jimbo walked to the bar and poured himself a shot of bourbon. He was about to have an anxiety attack and needed chemical aid. "We've lost our congressional backing, and the news media is baiting the waters so the sharks will eat. Are we going to respond or not?"

Amy followed the agitated CEO and tried to speak soothingly to him. "Not having the backing of Congress hurts us, there's no doubt. We have to play the cards we're dealt. I am preparing the press release we talked about. I have spoken with an agent from the FBI who is going to meet with the three of you individually. The press release, as we discussed, will outline your victim status. The impending legal matter prevents appearances and comments. This will buy you time and provide a benign response. We just need time for this to play itself out. Something more important will happen and trump this story, just give it time. Let's all just pray that Robin Hood M.D. goes away!"

# CHAPTER FOURTEEN

Samantha called her editor and CNN to arrange for dual coverage of the surrender. She wanted to have print and cable coverage of the event. She wanted a media empire like CNN to owe her. She thought again about the strange call from Robin Hood M.D. and feared that it was a joke. She considered having the police trace the number, but elected not to do so. This exclusive story would catapult her career, if she could get the kidnapper to talk.

She elected to position the news crew outside of the police station in hopes of obtaining an interview before the surrender. Of course, she did not know what this guy looked like. He had a very nice voice, very professional sounding, and she may well be able to recognize it if she were able to speak to him. It was not unusual for the press to work on stories outside of the precinct, so the satellite truck wouldn't attract undue attention.

At 8 pm, a Jaguar pulled into an available parking space located in front of the police station. A man stepped out and reached into the back seat of the vehicle. He pulled out a white lab coat and put it on. It extended below his knees. He straightened the collar and buttoned the coat.

Samantha watched the man with very little interest at first. When he put on his lab coat, she reached over and tapped the CNN reporter on the shoulder. "Turn on the camera," she instructed.

As the man reached the steps of the station, Samantha walked quickly towards him. She hadn't realized how tall he was from a distance. She couldn't quite reach high enough to tap him gently on the shoulder. "Sir, can I speak with you for a moment."

He turned and gazed down at her with piercing blue eyes. At six foot five, he towered over her. "Are you Samantha?"

"Yes sir, I am. Are you Robin Hood M.D.?"

"Yes I am. I am here to turn myself into the authorities. I want a trial."

He was a dignified-looking man. He wore wire framed glasses and a tweed suit. His name was embroidered in blue above his left coat pocket. An M.D. followed his name.

Samantha turned to the camera to make sure it was running. The CNN reporter was about to pounce with questions if Sam didn't hurry up and continue the interview.

"Are you a doctor?"

"Yes, I am."

"What kind of a doctor are you?"

"Family Practice."

"Did you kidnap the three CEOs?"

"Yes I did. I would have killed them if they had not agreed to help the patients."

Jennifer couldn't stand it any longer. She jumped ahead of Samantha, holding the CNN microphone in the doctor's face. "What is your name?"

"Dr. George Stanley." He reached for his lab coat and pointed at his name.

Samantha nudged Jennifer back away from the kidnapper. "Why did you kidnap and torture the CEOs? What were you trying to accomplish?"

"Americans are held hostage by health insurance companies. I wanted to start a revolution. I wanted to turn the tables, and show these multi-millionaires what it feels like to have your health in the hands of someone who is less than caring. I wanted to show them what powerlessness feels like."

Jennifer chimed in, "Why are you turning yourself in?"

"When you turn on a light, the cockroaches scurry for cover. A trial is the best way to shine light on this industry. I hope the congressmen follow through on their promise to hold hearings. If both occur, I pray a change will occur. I will finish out my part of the deal. That's enough with the questions. Let's go inside and get this started. Patients are suffering."

\* \* \*

Out of the blue, the prayers of the CEOs and their PR agent were answered. All it took was a tragic high impact celebrity story to divert attention away from the CEO kidnappings. It appeared, for the moment, that the country was more interested in where Anna Nicole was going to be buried, than in the well-being of insurance executives. Amy Nater and the three CEOs were watching CNN and celebrating with a bottle of Chardonnay as they watched the Anna Nicole debacle. This was a godsend. The timing was perfect.

That night Jimbo was the last to leave the television room. He sat glowing and basking in his momentary anonymity, unable to leave the TV. Just a short while ago, the TV had been his enemy...now it was his best friend and he didn't want to miss a moment. He drifted happily into champagne-induced dreams. He awoke when the programming was interrupted with a breaking news bulletin.

The anchor reached for his left ear, interrupting his dialogue with the CNN legal correspondent. "I'm sorry to interrupt Jane, but we have a breaking story."

"And now we'll go to CNN correspondent Jennifer Yo on site at the Atlanta Fulton County Police Department. She's there with Atlanta Journal Constitution reporter Samantha Huet. We have exclusive live footage of the surrender of Robin Hood M.D.."

He watched the broadcast initially in disbelief, then in horror. He began to shake uncontrollably. He threw his wine glass against the wall and screamed. The others came running.

"What in the hell is wrong with you?" Jonathan demanded.

"Look, damnit!" Jimbo pointed at the television. A man wearing a doctor's lab coat was standing in front of a police officer's desk.

Amy bit her fist. "Damn!" All four of them watched in horrified silence.

The audio of the correspondent roared through the room as Amy turned up the volume. "Dr. George Stanley, or as he has been calling himself, Robin Hood M.D., is approaching the police desk to turn himself in for the kidnappings of the CEOs of three major health insurance companies. Why don't we listen in?"

"What is this?" asked the desk sergeant, sitting behind a large elevated desk. "Is it Halloween or something? Did someone call a doctor?" he asked the officer behind him. He had not yet spotted the cameras and reporters in the background.

"I'm Robin Hood M.D.. I'm here to turn myself in for the kidnappings of the three CEOs."

"Yeah, and I'm Superman. Now you'd better get yourself back to the hospital where you belong. We are real busy down here tonight, Doc." He turned back to his reports and out of the corner of his eye noticed the media for the first time. 'What are those cameras doing here?"

"They're here to document my surrender. I'm Dr. George Stanley. I demand a trial for my crimes."

The desk sergeant stood up, realizing that he was actually on camera. "I'm sorry," he apologized to the camera and reporters: "I thought this was a joke. Guys around here are always playing jokes. I'll get a detective for you to talk to."

He walked quickly to the area behind the desk. He returned, with an embarrassed look on his face. He had not seen the news recently, so was unaware of the Robin Hood M.D. story. He saw so much bad at work, he sometimes took long vacations from watching TV and reading the paper, for his own sense of sanity. He presented the detective on duty, Harry Tern.

"Doctor, will you come with me please?" Detective Tern asked. The two disappeared down the corridor behind the desk.

The correspondent continued: "That had to be one of the most interesting candid moments I've seen. The officer thought this was a practical joke! However, this is no joke. It appears that Robin Hood M.D. is a physician named Dr. George Stanley. We haven't got much information on the doctor, but it appears that he's a family practice doctor who lives and practices in the Atlanta area. We'll be back when we get a statement from the Atlanta Police about the surrender."

The television room was completely silent as the four watched in various degrees of shock. Amy had a flood of emotions, as she realized that the CEOs were indeed toast. No two ways about it now. She wanted to cry but knew that she had to keep it together.

"What are we going to do now?" asked Theodore.

Amy poured herself another double espresso, trying to think of how to respond. She knew she was overdoing it with the caffeine, but drastic times called for drastic measures. She hoped she wasn't getting an ulcer. "If I'm reading this guy correctly, he wants to put the health insurance industry on trial, and he's willing to go to prison in order to do this. If he doesn't care what happens to him, and it appears he doesn't, he's dangerous foe. In the security circle, if a villain is willing to die in order to kill the one protected, he is a million times more dangerous."

Jimbo flinched at Amy's assessment of the situation and felt the now familiar knot of fear gnawing at his stomach. He watched Amy pacing around the room, trying to formulate her next move, and wondered bleakly what it would be like to escape to a remote tropical island and live out the rest of his days as a fugitive. "We have to prepare you all for a trial," Amy decided. "This is going to be ugly, guys, but I'll help you through each stage."

"I can't believe this shit!" shouted Jonathan. "I was the one kidnapped, and now I'm on the defensive. This is crazy!"

Amy tried to calm the three, "Stay in the moment. Nothing terrible has happened to us yet. Don't 'awfulize' the situation, as one of my friends calls it. Whenever we get bad news, we project the worst. We make things more terrible than they really are. Focus on what's right in front of you. And if it's bad, it won't always stay that way."

Theodore, still glued to the T.V. summonsed, "look! It's coming back on." Reluctantly, and trying not to "awfulize," the rest of the group quieted and turned back to the television.

"We're going back to our correspondent on the scene," the CNN anchor announced.

"We're waiting for a statement from the Chief of Police," the journalist boomed to the camera excitedly, trying to hide the hint of a smile. "Here he comes now."

The police department was now canvassed with media. They were drawn to the scene with what seemed a supernatural magnetic force. Some have referred to the onslaught of camera crews, reporters, helicopters, and vans with extended satellite transmitters as a circus. The streets near the Fulton County jail could more appropriately be described as a disorganized 'running of the bulls.' When anyone approached the podium, a scurry of reporters would race for a position, or jockey to fight for the position that they already occupied. Camera people would literally knock each other out of the way in order to get a good picture. When someone was speaking or answering questions from the podium, it was survival of the fittest in the media crowd. If violence were necessary to nab the big story, then so be it.

The evolutionary chain was set as far as the large networks were concerned. The large network, cable, and newspaper conglomerates always got the front row seats. When patrons of a network news program turned on their television, they did not expect to see the backs of the heads of reporters; they wanted to see the breaking story wide and up close. The second tier press, on the other hand, had to 'fight it out' to get the best shots. They would slip a microphone into an interview whenever they could. On occasion, a large media representative would get pushed to the back, but this was unusual. If it happened with any frequency, someone would lose their job.

The Chief avoided looking directly into the camera, and spoke in a way that betrayed his lack of patience with the media hounds which hovered around him. "At 8 pm, Dr. George Stanley turned himself into our custody. He claims to be Robin Hood M.D.. He's being interviewed at the present time. He's electing to act as his own counsel." He turned abruptly and walked away from the barrage of questions being hurled at him. He answered none of them. He didn't even bother raising a hand to halt them. His work would be so much easier without having to deal with the media pounding down the doors. He hoped this Robin Hood fiasco would just disappear, but he had a feeling it was only going to get worse before it got better.

\*    \*    \*

Dr. Susan Harrison had only ten minutes before leaving for the hospital. She was trying to quickly chop up a tomato for a quick salad, and her cat kept hopping on the counter, brushing up against her hands and getting in the way of the knife. "Cat, stop it! What's with you?" she snapped, swiping him off the counter again. She had never given her cat a name, other than 'Cat,' since she was sure her cat never thought of her as anything other than 'Human,' or at most 'Human who feeds me.' She liked the company of her cat just fine, normally. He kept her from feeling the loneliness of choosing a career over a family. And cats weren't as needy as dogs. A cat was a perfect companion for a busy surgeon. Lately though, Cat was acting differently. Susan wondered if it was because of George. Maybe the cat was sensing that he was gradually being replaced by another man. It was true, she and George were starting to get close; closer than she'd been to anyone in a long time. Was it possible that this confirmed bachelorette was starting to soften? She hated to admit it, but she had even caught herself daydreaming about what life with George might be like, and for the first time she felt her biological clock ticking.

She switched the small TV on the kitchen counter hoping to distract herself from such unwelcome thoughts as she went back to work on her salad. She caught just the tail end of the brief statement made by the Chief of Police. She stopped cutting and turned toward the small television. Had she heard correctly? No, she couldn't have heard it… but yes, there it was again. The commentators were talking about her boyfriend, classifying him as Robin Hood M.D.. She spoke aloud, "Robin Hood is a female. What the hell is going on? She passed me a note in the restroom!" She dropped her knife and gasped, "Oh my God, it was him. George passed me the note in the bathroom. He knew I was in there, waited until the bathroom emptied, and then he passed me the note. And of course, he knew about the case… I had just finished telling him. What the hell is he doing?" In a daze, she dropped to a counter-side kitchen stool. "George," she sighed as she absently stroked her cat, "What the hell are you doing?"

\* \* \*

The CEOs returned to their respective homes in great frustration. Any hopes that this story was going away or would be circumvented by a juicier story were long lost. A doctor kidnapping three health insurance company chief executive officers was a lead story, period, no matter what else was going on.

Amy was the last to leave the beach house. She wanted some time alone to think about what in the world to do next.

The FBI was followed into the police station by the entire world. Soap operas, daytime court television shows, and game shows were interrupted in order for the world to watch any event that went on in front of the police station. Announcers would state the most obvious of facts over and over as the world watched the most mundane of events unfold. Viewers continuously complained about the interruption of their favorite shows, but stayed glued to the set awaiting the unfolding of every detail.

"It appears that the FBI is now involved in the case. Three agents have entered the police station, where Dr. George Stanley, also known as Robin Hood M.D., awaits arraignment," the Fox News anchor reported. Live footage showed Dr. Stanley sitting alone in an interrogation chamber, looking calm and at peace.

"Dr. Stanley, can I get you anything to drink or eat?" asked Terrence Gunther, the District Director of the FBI.

"I'll take a cup of coffee."

Immediately, the door opened and a police officer appeared with a cup of coffee. George knew he had company on the other side of the glass wall.

"You claim to have kidnapped Theodore Bexley, Jr., Jonathan Willingham, and James Simmons. Is that the truth, or is this some sort of stunt to get back at the insurance companies?"

"It is the truth. I know you've seen the video I sent to the reporters!"

"You're here to turn yourself in?"

"I am, and as I've told the police officer who read me my rights, I do not want a lawyer."

The two FBI agents looked at each other as if they'd just heard someone ask to be voluntarily executed. The police detective had done a thorough interview, but they needed to hear this for themselves.

"I demand a trial with a jury of my peers."

The two agents stepped out of the room, excusing themselves. They discussed the notes and videos of the prior interviews, and elected not to reinvent the wheel by doing another exhaustive interview. They had enough evidence and a confession. They looked in the direction of the district attorney, who was watching from behind the window. He approached the agents with a confident stride.

"Henry, you heard him say that he wants a trial," Mr. Gunther announced to the approaching D.A.

"He'll get one, alright," Henry Turner, the Fulton County District Attorney announced, in a deep Southern drawl. "What he wants is a circus! He wants to put the CEO's of the insurance companies on trial. Well, he is in for a surprise. I will put his ass in jail until 'pigs fly.' He picked the wrong district to have this shindig in."

# CHAPTER FIFTEEN

———•●○▷◁●•———

Henry Turner called a meeting in his office for the next morning. All of his assistants were present along with two eager law clerks.

"Who is our judge?" asked the DA.

"Rudy Armstrong, the third," answered the assistant DA, Jenny Pointer.

"Is it Christmas, or just my lucky day?" the DA pronounced. "Has the judge assigned him counsel since he refused an attorney initially?"

"He's determined to act as his own attorney. He won't have it any other way," Mrs. Pointer responded.

Henry Turner stood and looked at everyone in the room: "This is either my time to shine or I have grabbed a tiger by the tail." He had a scornful look upon his face as he paced silently around the gathered legal team. "This guy is not stupid. He's likely crazy, but he has been very clever in his endeavors thus far. He has swayed public opinion and driven the media like a cattle rancher." He noticed a group gathered outside of his office window. "Look what we have here!" he waved the staff over to the window.

Protesters had gathered outside of the DA's office. They were carrying signs and walking in circles. The signs read: *Free Robin Hood. We need Health Insurance Reform. Arrest the CEOs and free Robin Hood. We need Health Care Reform.*

Henry turned to his staff, "It's looking like I may have a tiger by the tail."

*   *   *

Henry's Turner's wife was 45 and had minimal interest in sex. Henry was 46, but happened to have the sex drive of a 16 year old. This situation did not 'cut it' for the DA. Being married and having a girlfriend was a lot of work, but worth the effort. He needed a wife to advance his political career, and a girlfriend to advance his sexual desires. Although the arrangement was dangerous, it formed a balance in Henry's life that was requisite.

Jenny was beautiful. Her auburn hair and green eyes accentuated her dark complexion. Her descent was Mediterranean and her accent was Southern. She had a college degree and a humorous wit about her. Henry couldn't stand to be around anyone stupid, even if it was only for sex. Being 20 years her senior gave him a definite advantage in the conversation, and a back ache in the bedroom. They met at his office and he quickly seduced her. She had been hired as a secretary. He promised her a raise to quit her job and become his mistress. Another employee asked if she had been, "laid off," once, as she was sorely missed at the office. He found the phrasing of the question quite appropriate.

"Henry," Jenny called, in her sweet southern voice.

Henry turned over in the bed to face her, having fallen asleep as soon as the love making ended. "Yes, dear?"

"Are you going to treat Robin Hood as a criminal? He seems so noble and sophisticated. He's not a common criminal. How are you going to try him if he's just a good doctor trying to help his patients."

"He's not just a good doctor. He's a kidnapper too, for your information," Henry responded as he gazed in the beauty's direction. She shifted in the bed, and the glow of the moonlight outlined her barely subdued breasts undulating underneath the sheet. "Maybe he doesn't come across as a common criminal, but he is. There are no heroes any longer. Lofty motives do not justify violent criminal acts." *I may use something like that in my opening statement,* the D.A. thought to himself.

"My eyes are up here, sweetheart," she protested, changing the topic as she lifted his chin upwards to direct his gaze away from her large breasts and toward her eyes. "I'm thinking of having a breast reduction, what do you think?" She pulled down the cover and pushed her breasts together. "A woman with large breasts is never taken seriously!"

Henry shot straight up in bed and proclaimed in his most convincing courtroom voice: "Your honor, I make a motion to outlaw breast reduction surgery. It is unconstitutional! I take women with large breasts very seriously."

"Come here, you nut," Jenny pulled the prosecutor's head down towards her breast, as a nursing mother would an infant.

✻   ✻   ✻

All stood at attention as Judge Rudy Armstrong III entered the courtroom.

"Be seated," the judge commanded, scanning the room and taking up his gavel.

Dr. George Stanley sat alone at the defense table. He was wearing his doctor's lab coat with a stethoscope in the pocket. He looked lonely.

No one felt lonely at the plaintiff table. The District Attorney and two assistant District Attorneys sat at the table. Directly behind the table in the front row of the courtroom sat the two law clerks. A wooden rail was all that separated the clerks from the table. The law clerks would be working behind the scenes at all hours of the night. Their job was to memorize any law case related to ongoing motions, as the lawyers had long since forgotten them. To an onlooker they seemed only to serve as students; however, they were an integral, albeit anonymous, part of the team. The courtroom was empty otherwise.

"This looks like a mismatch," the judge assessed the imbalance of power in his courtroom. The judge looked at a document on the bench. "Dr. Stanley, you have never been convicted of a felony, never been convicted of a misdemeanor, never had a speeding ticket, never had an unpaid parking ticket, you pay your taxes on time; and yet, you sit alone before this court, having confessed kidnapping three men, and are demanding a trial at which you will have no lawyer."

The doctor stood, "Yes, your Honor. That is all true."

"Since you do not have counsel, I wish to assist you in your pleading. If you plead 'guilty,' you do not get a trial, only a sentence hearing. If you plead 'not guilty,' you get a trial. However, you have confessed to the crimes already."

The judge thought for a moment and looked at the prosecution table and then at the defendant. Henry Turner looked down at his hands and pushed his fingertips together disapprovingly. He was pissed that the judge was helping the doctor.

"I plead not guilty, I want a trial."

"A plea of 'not guilty' will go on record," the judge began to strike the gavel and then stopped, holding it in mid-air. "Dr. Stanley, I don't know what you have in mind, but allow me to educate you. This is my court room. You may have command of an operating room, but you do not know how a courtroom operates. How do you plan to manage a trial without any legal help?"

"My defense is simple. I don't need a lawyer."

"Maybe so, but I will not allow you to make a mockery of lady justice. Lawyers hate my courtroom. I am very strict with the rules of law. Do you have any legal training, whatsoever?"

"No, sir."

"Did you hear what I said about the rules of law?"

"Yes, sir."

"How do you intend to follow those?"

"I have a friend who is a paralegal with trial experience. She has agreed to walk me through the legal process."

"What is her name?"

"Alice Hendricks. She's worked at Walker, Moore, and Hearn for years."

"Yes, I suppose Alice will be of some help to you. She's very capable. I've read many briefs with her name on them. I want her to sit with you during the trial. Is that okay with you, Mr. Turner?"

"I prefer that he has proper legal counsel, but this is better than the fiasco we would have without any counsel."

"Now, to the matter of bail."

Dr. Stanley rose again, "Your honor, I refuse bail. I want to stay in jail!"

No one knew exactly how to respond.

Henry Turner rose and straightened his coat. "Your honor, this is a bizarre case, to say the least. This is the beginning of, what I predict, will be one scheme after another to put the health insurance industry on trial. He wants to be a martyr."

"Do you want to be a martyr, Dr. Stanley?"

"I am only interested in justice, your honor."

"One more thing, Doctor. You are not to dress in a lab coat in my court room. This would prejudice the jury, as it would in the other direction if you were in shackles. You are to wear a coat and tie for the proceedings," the judge instructed.

The doctor thought to himself, *I will wear what I damn well please. What is he going to do, put me in jail?*

"Thank you, your honor," Mr. Turner half stood and then sat back in his chair.

"The bail is set at $500,000. We'll have a trial date of July 21st. The court is adjourned."

Dr. Stanley was escorted to the van by two armed officers. They had befriended the doctor, and were pleased to receive some free medical advice for themselves and their families. At six foot four, George towered over the officers. His muscular build made the officers' lack of fitness even more obvious. The van passed the sea of media. George smiled to himself as he noted the protestors' signs.

"Free Robin Hood," a deputy laughed as he read one of the protest signs.

He had asked for the deputy to loosen the handcuffs, and he had done so. He had not been in handcuffs since the interrogation phase of Navy Seal training. His smile faded as he thought of Susan. He hoped she understood, but doubted that she would. She would probably try to bail him out. He, of course, would refuse. He was willing to trade his relationship, his freedom, and his medical license for justice. The State Medical Board had sent him a certified letter stating that his license was suspended pending investigation. He had told a guard that: "they can stick it up their ass!"

His wife, Sheila, had died of breast cancer ten years previously. Her oncologist wanted to try an experimental therapy, but the insurance company had refused to pay for it because it had not been identified as a standard treatment. He was a medical student at the time, and could not afford the $15,000 fee for each dosage of medication. He was assured that it probably would not have worked anyway. He fumed as he thought of how many patients receive the treatment and survive today. *It would have saved Sheila's life,* he thought. *What board protects patients from insurance companies?*

"Almost home, Doc," the guard startled George out of his trance.

"Home," Dr. Stanley laughed as he said the word.

The van pulled past another set of protestors as it entered the underground garage at the Fulton County jail. The group recognized the van and screamed encouragement to Robin Hood M.D.. The doctor changed into his orange jumpsuit and headed for his cell. He lay down and picked up the *National Geographic* he'd left on his bed. He had earmarked a page to mark his place and began to read. His busy medical practice didn't allow for leisure time, so George asked for magazines to read, taking advantage of the 'down time.'

"Doc, you have a visitor," summoned the guard.

Dr. Stanley was escorted to the visitors' area. Unlike the set-up typically seen in television dramas, this was simply a room with table and chairs. There were no glass windows requiring telephones to speak through. Dr. Susan Harrison entered the room. *I'm going to miss that,* he thought to himself, noticing her shapely legs exposed to the knee beneath her skirt.

"Do you have anything to say?" asked the irritated brain surgeon.

"Yes I do, according to *National Geographic,* every year more New Yorkers are bitten by humans than beachgoers around the world are bitten by sharks."

"Damnit, this is not funny. I would slap the shit out of you, if I weren't afraid they'd keep me here!"

"I need the company, and it's not funny; *National Geographic* is a serious magazine."

"George, did you lose your mind? I didn't, I mean, I don't want you to go to jail; I mean prison, for the rest of your life. When I told you about Natasha, I didn't mean for you to do something like kidnap the CEO of her insurance company. You followed me into the ladies' room, for God's sake! All this time I thought Robin Hood was a female."

Susan willed herself not to cry. She would NOT allow him to see how weak she felt. She would not give in to tears. She tried to summon all her anger so she could shut down the aching of her heart. "Why did you do this?" she demanded furiously, trying to blink back the tears. "I wanted to marry you and have your children, not visit you in a prison!"

"I did what had to be done!" Dr. Stanley argued. "I let them kill my wife, so that the insurance company could improve their profit for the quarter." Susan looked startled. George realized how harshly he had just spoken, and softened his tone of voice as he explained what had happened to Sheila. "The more patients I saw receiving the drug that she had been denied, the more angry I became. Timothy Sims, the young man whose insurance company refused to pay for the bone marrow transplant, was initially a patient of mine. You're familiar with that situation aren't you?"

"Yes, I watch the news. That was ridiculous."

"My partner is Debra Justin's doctor. The insurance company labeled her diabetes as a pre-existing condition, nearly costing her life." Dr. Stanley paused for a minute and then continued: "It all came together. I was watching these innocent patients suffer all around me. The memory of my wife's suffering plagued me with every breast cancer patient I saw survive. I'm happy that they are doing well, but I'm enraged that I had to lose my wife unnecessarily."

Sorry for what she hadn't known, Susan bowed her head. She had never heard the story of how he lost his wife. In fact, she realized she'd never heard George talk about anything personal. He was normally so stoic. It was easy to assume that nothing ever got to him. "Well, you've certainly got people's attention! You're making headlines everywhere. They had your picture from the Navy Seals on CNN yesterday. I didn't know you were in the special forces."

"I was on a Seal team for six years. I was stationed in Hawaii for the last two years."

Susan reached for George's hand and began to rub it. The somnolent guard stepped forward admonishing them, "You're not allowed to touch."

Susan folded her hands. "I need to go. I'll support you all the way through this. You really are a Robin Hood, and I'm very proud of you. I just hope you're able to pull it off and help all those patients out there."

"Do you really want to have my….."

"We will discuss it when you are a free man."

The two arose and looked toward the guard.

"You can give him a little kiss, but no hugging or touching," he allowed.

Susan gave George a quick kiss on the lips. "I love you. Don't do anything stupid."

George gave her a wink and smiled.

\* \* \*

Henry Turner had never prosecuted a case like this. He wasn't sure what to do. Public sentiment seemed to be in favor of this nutcase doctor. It was, however, a very difficult thing to measure. You couldn't exactly take a poll, could you? The case seemed simple enough, but many very tangled labyrinths looked simple initially, becoming more and more complicated as time went on. The more he thought about it, the more concerned he grew. He would feel better if the guy had proper representation. There was something to be said for predictability. If you could, with some certainty, predict what your enemy was going to do, you could plan for battle. If you had no idea of how they were going to fight you, even if you were the far superior warrior, you were at somewhat of a disadvantage. You don't know which weapons to fight with. This was why terrorists were so effective. Henry suspected that Dr. Stanley knew this as well as he.

"Do you guys think they'll make a motion to suppress the confession?" Henry Turner asked, as the meeting with his staff began.

The assistant DA began: "I have no idea, but if they decide to do so, they will be successful. The doctor made his confession three hours before he was read his rights."

"Son of a bitch!" Henry shouted, slamming his fist on the table. "I've told them time and again to just go ahead and immediately read the rights to anyone even thinking about making a confession! This could put us in a bad situation if they're able to have the confession thrown out. Those morons could screw up a two car funeral, I swear." The DA's face was now red.

"The good news is that no motions have been filed, and that Robin Hood, what is it, M.D., wants to be in jail. He's made that very clear to everyone," Junior Barnett pointed out.

Mrs. Pointer, the other assistant DA asked: "I wonder how much influence the paralegal has on the doctor? Maybe we can influence her to help us by structuring his defense in a format we're accustomed to."

"You can bet your ass and the barn door that he's planning on being as unstructured as possible. That's his defense. He's a Navy Seal. I saw a picture in a magazine once advertising for these guys. It was a picture of tumble weeds, fractioned into labeled frames. Each was labeled with a time. The 15 frames represented the lapse of about a minute of time. I looked at it for five minutes before I realized that two of the tumbleweeds in the forefront of the photograph were missing from the last two frames. If you had been an enemy strolling along through the desert, you would have been dead before you knew what hit you. He thrives on non-structure and surprise. He was trained to operate as the underdog. I don't care if he's a doctor or not, once a Seal always a Seal. Look what he did to the CEOs! He scared them so badly they're still afraid to say anything!" Henry Turner insisted.

The law clerks looked like deer in headlights. Law School had not prepared them for this type of a case. It was not until this case that they realized how luxurious it was to sit back in a case and watch, instead of running to the law library and computer every time a motion was made.

"Damned if I'm going to sit around and twiddle my thumbs, but I guess there's nothing to do but wait and see what happens." Henry grumbled.

An unfamiliar voice resounded from the back of the room. Clerks were supposed to be seen, preferably in the library, and not heard. Arnold could not resist asking the looming question hovering over the case, "Are you going to call the CEOs as witnesses?" His partner almost wet his pants in disbelief. He elbowed him as people began to turn to see who asked the question.

Henry Turner decided against ripping the student's head off, and instead used this for a teaching moment. "How do you think we should proceed, young man? Stand up and present your argument to the group."

"Thank you sir," the student arose and walked to the podium. "It is, indeed, a complex matter. The defendant would love to call the three CEO's as witnesses, but cannot; because number one, he's allegedly the kidnapper, and number two, the rules mandate that in a criminal case, this is the decision of the prosecutor."

The student paced away from the podium with the sway of a seasoned prosecutor. He quizzically stroked his chin, as any great thinker would, and gave a dramatic pause. He then continued: "I think that the doctor is assuming we're going to have to call the CEO's. We're assuming that the doctor wants the CEOs on the stand, and we have to look at the risk versus the benefits. The risk is turning this case into a trial of the health insurance industry, which would certainly pose Robin Hood M.D. in good standing, robbing the rich company and giving to the poor patients. The already elevated public sentiment for this criminal could rise even further. The benefits would be that we could 'lawyer up,' and prevent him from asking irrelevant questions of the witnesses. His paralegal wouldn't be able to keep up with all of the objections and motions. Every question would meet a flurry of objections. We could even try to make the judge ask the questions in cross examination, because the CEO's are horrified of this animal. He nearly killed one of the guys, reportedly."

Henry Turner stood as the law clerk found his seat. He walked to the window and looked at the protestors. Turning to the group at the table, he began: "I am damn impressed with your assessment, son. You show a great deal of insight. We can use some of that around here. Come and sit at the table with us."

Arnold Kirk did as he was told, leaving his fellow clerk in the back of the room.

The DA continued: "This young clerk has outlined a crisis point that we are going to have to cross, and soon. I'm not sure how to approach this, but Mr. Kirk is correct in his summation of this mess, that we are going to have to weigh the pros and the cons. Is it worth it to bring in the CEOs or can we just use their depositions? We need to formulate a plan."

\* \* \*

Amy Nater had had some tough assignments in the past, but never one as terrible as this. She had to either drop this PR assignment or use drastic measures to make some attempt at 'righting the sinking ship.' This had been done in the past. Some activities went on in the agency that went unspoken. Bribery and blackmail were not discussed at staff meetings, but she had heard of, and personally knew of a few drastic cases in which they had to get into the trenches to save a client. This did not happen often, but it was going to happen in this case….she had no choice…And she had a feeling that she wouldn't have to look too far to dig up some valuable dirt.

Amy did not attribute anything except a memory store of useless religious trivia to her good Christian upbringing. When asked, she was known to jokingly refer to herself as a "recovering Catholic," not willing to acknowledge how deeply her sense of morality hinged on biblical teachings. She thought of herself as extremely liberal, but had never rid herself of the prodigal Catholic guilt regarding "sex, drugs, and rock n' roll." However, she was rationally minded enough to recognize that it wasn't just the Catholic rearing that shaped her sense that sex was somehow a deviant activity. It permeated the whole of western culture. And in this case, it was a very good thing that it did.

Amy was pleased with the findings of the private detective she hired to follow the District Attorney, the most significant item of interest being Jenny. It brought to mind the story in the Old Testament, of King David happening upon the beautiful Bathsheba bathing in the nude, and liking what he saw, deciding to take her as his own. The fact that she was married was only a minor setback, resolved by arranging for a frontline (suicidal) military assignment for her unfortunate husband. He created a widow in order to make a wife.

Amy doubted if Henry had first spotted Jenny bathing in the nude, but she couldn't help but think of an analogy as she viewed the photographs taken by the PI. The 'Legal King' of Fulton County was willing to trade his empire for sex, just as King David had been. Two thousand years later, and the story remained the same. Sex ruled the world. The most powerful of men all seemed to have the greatest weakness for sex. The greatest minds allowed the most primitive workings of their brains to rule their lives, and in many cases ruin them. Unconscious yearnings always overruled conscious, rational objections.

Henry Turner would take care of the CEOs by dropping all charges against Robin Hood M.D., or by not putting them on the stand. Either that or he was about to take an ugly fall. This show had to stop. She was not going to allow the health insurance industry to be placed on trial in a Kangaroo Court. She had learned that the kidnapping doctor was to act as his own attorney! He would be cross examining her clients on National and International television. *Bullshit,* she surmised. *I will make this problem, maybe not disappear, but look a hell of a lot more like an empty bubble.*

# CHAPTER SIXTEEN

"Do you wish to make a motion to suppress your confession?" asked the paralegal. "My guess, from what you've explained to me about when the cops read you your rights, is that you can have the confession thrown out."

"No, the confession will stay as it is."

Alice took off her thick, black-rimmed glasses and wearily rubbed her eyes before looking the doctor in the eyes. "Do you care if you go to prison for the next 30 years or so?"

"My life is over. If I can help people not have to go through what my wife and I had to endure, then so be it. Throw the keys away."

"Do you want to put up any fight at all?"

"Not unless it helps us expose the health insurance industry."

"As a paralegal, I'm obliged to fight with all of my abilities to retain your freedom. This defense of no defense and, let's be frank, martyrdom, is unacceptable. I'll have to consult with the judge."

"As you wish, but my only fight will be with the insurance companies. I'll do more damage to them by making the District Attorney drag the CEOs through a trial. Just having those bastards on television will help the public push for reform. Not defending myself against the prosecution will make me look like a victim, which is what I need to happen if I'm going to fight the industry. I'm going to have to say I'm guilty of the crime, and I'll need the support of public opinion. This can't be a half-witted effort!

"But you pleaded not guilty!"

"I had to in order to have a trial. The longer we're on television, the more negative exposure the health insurance industry gets. And the prosecutors won't know what in the hell to do with me. Nothing beats the element of surprise when waging battle, like when my Seal team crept into a terrorist camp and killed their leader in his sleep. The only one who knew we were there was the dead man. The sun rose and panic set in. We left a small American flag underneath his pillow, as a reminder to the survivors, of the power and stealth of their sworn enemy."

"Well, Doctor, it appears that you've thought this all out," the paralegal relented, shaking her head. "I'll notify the judge that I'm not allowed to do my job. I do hope that at some point you'll let me help you, or hire a lawyer. I'm afraid that you underestimate Henry Turner. I've seen him at work, doctor. He'll bury you alive."

\* \* \*

Jennifer Meers was startled by the knock at the door. She was always startled by the door when sitting at her computer...the only place she could fit her desk was on the wall opposite the entrance. The apartment was small, but she couldn't complain...it was paid for by Henry Turner. As promised, she was paid a salary, so she didn't need to work. She wanted to be a writer, and was currently researching a book. She had graduated with a political science major, which meant that she had to work menial jobs while deciding whether to apply to law school or graduate school. This new 'career move' had allowed her time to do what she wanted. Henry did not ask for much of her time, and she enjoyed the time they did spend together. She was pragmatic about the arrangement, and did not mind being a 'kept' woman while she was planning her next move.

Jennifer opened the door with wallet in hand, sure that it must be the Chinese food she'd ordered. The woman at the door, however, did not appear to have any hint of 'lo mein' or 'chicken fried rice' about her.

"Are you Jennifer Meers?"

"Yes, I am. What can I help you with?"

"I have a business proposition for you." Amy Nater handed over a file to Jennifer. "May I come in to talk with you about it?"

Jennifer hesitated a moment, but then decided it was safe to allow her into the apartment. "Come in."

\* \* \*

Serving on Jury duty has been described by some as an activity for people too stupid to get out of serving, or for people who had nothing better to do with their time. All sides begged for jurors who were in neither category. Attorneys everywhere have been known to plead any intelligent citizen willing to listen, that if called for duty: to "Please, please, please serve on the jury."

Many jurisdictions had cracked down on people skipping out of jury duty. The honorable Rudy Armstrong had served enough bench warrants for non-attendance to get the community's attention. He did not care what you were doing; you were going to be present when he called you! The typical excuses of being a student or having a small child did not fly in his court room. If you were sick, you had to have a written excuse from a doctor. He would sometimes call the doctor and verify the medical problems. He once put a young mother in jail for lying to him about a medical condition. More pre-trial cross-examination of called jurors had occurred in Judge Rudy Armstrong's court than in any other in the county.

The potential jurors had been provided with a questionnaire to be filled out prior to presentation. Many brought the questionnaire unprepared, or did not bring it at all. The questions were all from the prosecutor, as the defendant demanded to question all potential jurors. The judge was fuming.

"Son, this trial will take us two years to complete at this pace. Now, I'm sorry, but you'll just have to follow protocol here so we can keep things moving along."

"Yes sir," the doctor answered: "I understand. I have a questionnaire ready to give to the potential jurors." He handed the paperwork over to the judge.

The judge glared over his glasses at Dr. Stanley when he finished reading the prepared questions. "For the sake of time, I want you to read your questions to a room full of jurors. You can separate the jurors, if you wish, according to their answers. You get to choose the 6 jurors that you want. You do this by choosing your own, or by striking a prosecutor's choice. Do you understand how to choose your jurors?"

"Yes sir, I do."

The process began immediately, with the defendant, Dr. George Stanley, reading his questions to the potential jurors. As far as he was concerned, the most important question was whether they had health insurance or not. He knew that 90% of people had some conflict with their health insurance company. If he could get a jury with 75% of the people insured, he would win the case. All he had to do was remind the jurors that *THIS COULD HAPPEN TO THEM OR THEIR FAMILIES!*

To separate out the desirable jurors, George looked for positive responses to questions such as: "How many of you have health insurance? Have any of you had an insurance company refuse to pay for a treatment, study, or a medication? Have any of you had a family member harmed by an insurance company? Do you feel that, under certain circumstances, violent and revolutionary acts are required to effect a change?"

He looked for negative responses to questions such as: "Do you work for an insurance company? Do you have family members who work for insurance companies? Do you feel that lawsuits against insurance companies have a negative impact on society as a whole? Do you feel that vigilante or revolutionary acts are never justified, no matter what the crime is?"

Obviously, Henry Turner fought to make the jury favorable for the accusers. That was his job. George could tell the DA was nervous. George looked at this like a Texas Hold 'em game with very high stakes. He made every attempt to keep his own cool and not let on how nervous he, himself, was. Every time he lost a juror he really wanted, he willed himself to keep up the poker face.

"I can't get a read on exactly what he's looking for," the DA confided to the law clerk he'd taken under his wing. "His questions are obvious, and frankly, too very much to the point. The jurors who want to please him and get on the jury, are easy to spot. Of course, those are the ones we fight the hardest to keep off, using our vetoes if need be. However, we know he's an ex-Seal, so he's a master of subtlety. There's more here than meets the eye; I'm sure of it. He'll be tougher to beat than it appears.

All he needs is one sympathetic juror to push his agenda through the other eleven."

Jury selection ended with the prosecution seemingly more satisfied with the selection than the defense. The judge and paralegal had had to assist the doctor with all of the motions, which delayed the proceedings. By the time the process concluded, the kidnapper seemed a little rattled.

\* \* \*

Amy followed Jennie the several steps into the quaint little kitchen and sat down at the table as instructed. *This lady was beautiful. Pictures did not do her justice,* she thought. *No wonder he strayed out of the yard... this young lady was hot.*

Jennifer opened the folder she'd been handed. Enclosed were pictures of her and Henry Turner together in various public and private venues. "What is this?" Jennifer demanded, her perfect complexion flushing a deep crimson.

"A job proposal."

"I think you've made some kind of mistake. This isn't---"

"Your affair with Mr. Turner is interesting to my clients." Amy interrupted. "We are willing to pay you one million dollars to assist us in a case that Mr. Turner is currently prosecuting. We want to be sure that the CEOs in the kidnapping case are not put on the witness stand."

"How am I going to do that?"

"I'm sure you can be counted on to exercise your powers of persuasion," Amy suggested, leaning over the table to twirl a lock of Jennie's hair between her fingers. "We thought of other ways to handle our knowledge of Mr. Turner's misgivings. None of those would help you, and likely, none would help my clients as much as this little proposal. Turning a man when he doesn't know he's being turned is always preferable to twisting his arm to make him behave. One million dollars is a lot of money. It'd be a good start on your writing career."

"How am I going to influence him? He's a powerful man."

"Power is an illusion! The way I see it, you have all the power, not him. With those hips, you could make him prosecute the Mormon Tabernacle Choir."

"And if I don't take your proposal?"

"You're much too smart to believe this arrangement will last once his wife finds out about you." Amy pointed out coyly: "you lose the 'job' and all the frills that go along with it. You've tasted the spoils and I know you like what you've tasted. You can step into the big leagues with this kind of money. Invest it wisely, and never work again! Write for a living, and live on your interest. No more low wage jobs." Amy could tell she was getting through to the young woman, who rose and distractedly fussed with the coffee-maker on the counter. "Money is freedom. Don't let anyone tell you different."

"I'm still not so sure I can sway his decision," Jennie fretted.

"You can and you will. It's the only logical thing you can do. If worse comes to worse, contact me, and I'll help you. I've enclosed some personal information about Henry and his life that you're likely not privileged to. Use it as blackmail if need be, but only as a last resort."

# CHAPTER SEVENTEEN

The courtroom was filled to capacity. Outside, the number of protestors thronging the courthouse just barely surpassed the number of reporters. As usual, the volume of reporters exponentially exceeded the number necessary to report the story. Anyone entering or leaving the courtroom was almost obscenely harassed by the media.

The protestors had become increasingly vocal, and provided even more fuel for the news hungry mobs of media...especially when people not normally accustomed to protesting came out of the woodworks to rally in support of Robin Hood M.D.. An aging hippy picketing the evils of modern society hardly caused any reporter to more than bat an eyelid, but put the picket sign in the hands of a grandmother and then you had a story.

"I think Robin Hood is a good man and a good doctor," a 90 year old woman shouted in a voice surprisingly shrill for such a frail body. She had a *free Robin Hood* sign in her right hand, and a King James Bible in her left. When asked to comment for Channel 11 Action News, she let them have an earful: "Those insurance companies only care about money! They don't care about the patients. They collect the premiums, but don't want to pay the bills. My son had to file bankruptcy because his insurance company wouldn't pay up. May these executives burn in hell for it."

\*   \*   \*

"All rise, for the honorable Judge Rudy Armstrong." The mass of people in the courtroom did as commanded, with a great swell of chatter and musings amongst themselves. The judge approached the bench and pounded his gavel to bring order to the raucous scene.

"Be seated. We have a large crowd and the media present for the case of the State of Georgia versus Dr. George Stanley. I will have zero tolerance for outbursts from the crowd. I want the courtroom as quiet as it is at midnight, or I will vacate it. I find it unusual that no motions were made by the defense. Did your paralegal discuss with you a motion to suppress your confession, Dr. Stanley?"

Dr. Stanly stood: "I discussed this with her, and I do not want the confession suppressed."

The judge stared at Robin Hood for a long 30 seconds. "I don't quite know why you would want to shoot yourself in the foot, but that is your choice. I do warn you, however, as I have previously, that I will not have any shenanigans in my court room. Did we not discuss your attire during your arraignment?"

"Yes sir, we did."

"What is it that you have on today?"

"Surgical scrubs. Your honor, this is what I wear to work. I don't wear a suit and tie. I am not, and do not want to look like a lawyer, no offense."

"Oh, well." The judge looked over the end of his bifocals; "None taken. They come in my courtroom with suits on that cost more than my first house. However, I want you to wear attire that doesn't potentially sway the jury. Understood?"

"Yes sir."

The judge turned to the jury box. "Ladies and gentlemen of the jury, I wish to instruct you in this case. Dr. Stanley has elected, against my advice, to serve as his own attorney. Furthermore, he is putting up little defense, but demands a trial by jury. He is aware of how unwise this is. Now he may try to convince you to side with him on grounds outside of the trial at hand. However, we are only interested in the facts of the case. You are only to consider the facts in this case in making your decision about guilt or innocence."

The judge turned to the plaintiff's table and raised his hand. "Let us begin this trial with the opening statements."

Henry Turner rose, buttoned his suit vest, and launched into his scathing assessment of the case at hand. He was a great orator, and on this occasion gave a grand performance. He pointed his finger in the face of Dr. Stanley five times during his 90 minute remark. Drawing to a close, he strolled confidently to the plaintiff's table, assured that he had put a huge damper on anything this nut was about to say. This was not the last time he was to underestimate his opponent.

Dr. Stanley rose, glaringly out of place in his green hospital scrubs. "How many of you have seen the movie *My Cousin Vinnie?*"

Seven jurors timidly raised their hands.

"Do any of you recall what the defense's opening statement was?"

One of the jurors stifled a chuckle as he recalled the line Joe Pesci uttered upon awakening to the Judge demanding an opening statement; "What that other guy said was all bullshit!"

"Objection!" Henry Turner roared, leaping to his feet.

"Approach the bench, both of you. Bring the paralegal, Doctor."

The judge put his hand over the microphone as the room buzzed with laughter.

"I did not see that movie," the judge admitted. "What was his opening statement?"

Henry Turner gave the 'Ole!' sign to the doctor. In a gravely serious fashion, Dr. Stanley enlightened the judge to the famous movie moment. The judge's face turned orange in anger.

"I will tell you this one more time. This is not a game. The only," the judge grasped the microphone with both hands and leaned closer to the three: "bullshit that will go on in my courtroom is what I allow, and Dr. Stanley, that is very little. You will sit down and not speak during your trial, unless you can come up with something better than this."

"Oh, yes sir."

"The jury will disregard Dr. Stanley's opening remarks. You may proceed, doctor, albeit carefully. Remember, you cannot say 'I did it,' or 'I am guilty,' or I will have to end the trial and move to the sentencing hearing. I am sure that the paralegal has advised you of this, but I want to again make this very clear to you."

Henry Turner was fuming that the judge had offered advice so freely to the doctor. He had hoped the idiot would stand up and say, 'I did it; now I want to show you why.'

"I want to use a defense opposite to the one in the movie." Dr. Stanley motioned.

The Judge drew in a quick breath and grabbed for his gavel. Before he could strike it, the defendant quickly completed his thought.

"I agree with everything Henry Turner said. Every word of it is true."

The courtroom buzzed as the judge gaveled in anger.

"I have no aspiration to be the next Judge Judy. I will clear this room if the outbursts continue. Camera or not, we will have order. Continue, but with care, Doctor."

"Thank you, your Honor. I want to focus this trial not on what I might have done, but why I might have done it. Whether you put me in jail for my possible crimes is up to you. I don't care either way."

The doctor slid his hand along the rail which separated him from the jury box and spoke softly. "What I care greatly about is that you and the remainder of the country learn what people go through in dealing with health insurance companies. Imagine paying a contractor to build you a house in advance, maybe on a monthly basis, and just as you are ready for him to come and begin the work he decides he's going to keep your money, but not do the work. What would you do? I imagine that eventually you would call the police. He would be arrested and go to jail. On the other hand, if this were a health insurance policy, not a thing would happen to the company. People pay premiums for years, only to learn that when they need a certain medication or procedure, they have to beg for it…And there's no guarantee it'll be granted. Folks, this happens every day to everyday Americans like you."

Sensing he was striking a chord with his audience, George visibly relaxed a little. Before continuing, he turned to look at the judge, who gave him a subtle nod of approval. It seemed that the judge was warming up to the cause which the doctor championed.

As George told the jurors about his wife's unnecessary death at the hands of the health insurance industry, he demanded such attention that one could have heard a pin drop, except for the occasional sound of a swallowed sob or sniffle. There was not a dry eye in the courtroom by the time he finished his personal story. He then explained in great detail the medical cases related to the kidnappings. He stopped and looked around at the tear-streaked faces. Deciding he'd said enough he drew his opening statement to a close and took a seat.

"We'll end here today and resume at nine in the morning," the judge gaveled more lightly than before as he rose and retreated to his chambers.

\* \* \*

"Mr. Turner, have you decided whether to put the CEOs on the stand?" asked Arnold Kirk, the favored law clerk (for the moment).

Henry could still smell the lingering aroma of Jennifer's cologne as he wiped a handkerchief across his sweating brow and contemplated a response. Her interest in the case was increasing, and her sharp intellect made it worthwhile to discuss the case with her. She made a compelling argument to leave the CEOs off the witness stand. He had a visceral, but ridiculous feeling that her love-making had been more passionate when he seemed in favor of keeping them off the stand.

"After much thought, I think it simpler not to place the victims on the stand. I think the doctor would turn this into more of a fiasco than it already is. We have a confession, and a video tape of the crime made by the criminal. I think that's enough. In fact, it may be too much. The evidence is so overwhelming that it seems that we have something missing."

"Why don't we bring in an insurance executive who has a gripe with doctors to counter some of the damaging statements Dr. Stanley is making about the health insurance industry?" offered Arnold.

"Yes, I'd thought of that and it seemed too obvious an attack at first, but now that you mention it, son, it may just work. I want you kids to find me a witness, and fast, who can do this for us. Get that Nater woman, you know, the public relations spokesperson for the three companies. She'll be an unapologetic bulldog on the stand."

\* \* \*

"Doctor, we have to talk about a motion we need to make regarding the videos the prosecution will show. I'm sure they won't allow the audio to be heard by the jury, or at the very least, try to leave out the statements that the CEOs read. We need the jury to hear the statement in order to have a fighting chance," the paralegal counseled.

"I agree. Have you thought about the defense I've proposed?"

"I think you have a good idea, but you have an uphill battle. You'll have to get the witnesses to answer in a way that fits exactly with your plan, if you want to cast any doubt in the jurors' minds."

George knew she was right. He knew it was a gamble, but knowing he had everything to lose, he had nothing to lose by trying.

\* \* \*

"All rise for the honorable Judge Rudy Armstrong."

Judge Armstrong approached the bench, motioned the courtroom to be seated, and immediately began the proceedings. "Doctor, I understand that you have a motion to prevent the prosecution from showing the video exhibit in any portion, except in total."

Dr. Stanley rose. He was wearing a coat and tie, but had surgical shoe covers on. The judge looked over his glasses at the shoes, but did not comment.

"Yes sir, they have to show it in total or not at all."

Henry Turner was standing as well. "We are not going to show the CEOs reading a statement that the kidnapper wrote. They were forced to read the statement. We propose deleting the audio from the statement."

"Motion is granted. Play the video in total."

"Your Honor, we would like to introduce Exhibit A."

Henry walked to the jury box. "Dr. Stanley has presented us with a video of the kidnappings. He made a statement to the police that he is the masked man in the video. A statement will be read by the three CEOs. These men were forced at gunpoint to read the statements. I do not want you to pay any attention to the statements."

"Objection, Your Honor."

"What is the objection, Doctor?"

"He's giving the jury instructions. Only you can do this."

"Objection sustained. The jury will disregard the instructions and decide what they, themselves, think of the video."

Dr. Stanley slid the legal pad back to his paralegal. She tore out the page with the words *objection, judge's instruction* written on it. He mouthed "thanks" to her.

The video was shown in its entirety to the jurors. Several had shocked looks on their faces as they listened to the statement incriminating the health insurance industry. One of the women on the jury continually glanced over at the doctor with a look of approval.

"In addition to the video evidence of the crime, we have a taped confession. This is Exhibit B. Your Honor, we would like to introduce Exhibit B."

"You may proceed."

The jury watched the video of the detailed confessions.

As soon as it ended, Mr. Turner immediately approached the bench. "Your Honor, we would like to call our only witness, Ms. Amy Nater."

Amy took the witness stand and was sworn in.

The prosecutor circled the witness stand like an outfielder circling a fly ball just before he snags it. He made eye contact with each and every juror before he asked the first question.

"What is your occupation, Ms. Nater?"

"I'm a public relations expert. I represent the three companies affected by the kidnappings."

"Isn't it true that you have expertise about the insurance industry?"

"Objection, leading question!" shouted Dr. Stanley.

"Sustained," Judge Armstrong agreed.

"I will rephrase the question. Tell the jury about your expert knowledge of the health insurance industry. In particular, tell us about the problems that the industry is having with unnecessary testing and prescribing, and how criminal doctors are draining the system."

George liked the first question better, but he felt empowered demanding that the DA rephrase his question.

"The health insurance industry is under attack for trying to stamp out fraud and abuse. We have to hire doctors in an attempt to confirm that expensive testing is necessary. Some doctors make up for a lack of knowledge by way of excessive testing. Instead of using conservative and cost effective measures to diagnose and treat, we have doctors ordering three thousand dollar MRIs, just because they have the technology available."

Henry was watching Dr. Stanley for his reaction. The DA hoped that the doctor would come unglued in front of the jury.

"All we hear is whining about why we don't allow doctors to order any and every test and drug they want to prescribe. The health insurance industry would soon perish if this were allowed."

"Does the industry have problems with doctors committing fraud?" the prosecutor proceeded.

The witness laughed. "They steal about half a billion dollars a year from patients. Overcharging patients, producing poor documentation, charging for procedures that were not done, even inventing fictitious patient write-ups…these are just a few of the tactics these low life doctors use in order to defraud the insurance companies and our clients. And then they have the nerve to cry foul when insurance companies enact rules to protect their very survival. Patients do not want their premiums wasted or stolen."

"Do doctors make more money from insurance companies or from government programs?"

"They make the majority of their money from the health insurance industry, though they often seem to forget this little detail, and are continually biting the hand that feeds them. They feel so omnipotent, that they fail to give us the most basic of courtesies. These guys really think they're Gods. I met a doctor once who said, 'When a patient prays to God before a procedure, who do you think that they are really praying to?' To make us seem the bad guys is ridiculous. If you don't like the health care industry now, just let doctors control it and see what a mess you'll have."

"Why do you think that a doctor would kidnap and torture the top executives of the insurance companies you represent?"

"He obviously has some type of mental disturbance. I would correlate his actions with those of abortion clinic bombers. They take drastic action which even the most staunch abortion critic abhors, and act justified in their crimes. They act as if they did everyone a favor. Dr. Stanley is no different. He is going to tell us how he was acting heroically in order to save the lives of the three patients."

"Are you scared of Dr. Stanley?"

"Only a fool wouldn't be scared of this maniac! Look at him. Look how large he is! Look at his athletic frame! A man of his build could be extremely dangerous if he put his mind to it…coupled with a vengeful psyche and military training, he could do serious damage to anyone who crossed him."

"Your Honor," Henry Turner turned to the judge and entreated, "I don't want the doctor to intimidate my witness. I ask that he stay at his table for his cross examination of Ms. Nater."

"Very well. Dr. Stanley, please ask your questions from the defense table."

George Stanley had been through interrogation training. He wasn't about to show any emotion to these neophytes. They had no idea what pressure was. While Henry was an experienced prosecutor, he had never been choked with barbed rope or punched in the gut because he had not spoken. George was sure it bothered the prosecution more that he had not objected, than if he had made multiple objections (as his paralegal had urged him to) during the direct examination. In fact he didn't so much as twitch an eyebrow, even during the most insulting of testimony.

Dr. Stanley remained seated as he began the cross examination. "Ms. Nater, what is your occupation?"

"Are you going to ask me the same questions?"

Dr. Stanley held his hand out to the judge.

"You will answer the questions that are posed to you," commanded Judge Armstrong.

"I'm a public relations officer, as I said earlier."

"Kindly tell the jury what it is that public relations officers do?"

"We generally assist companies in communicating with the public. We have too many functions to name, actually."

"Have you ever lied to the public to protect a company's reputation?"

Henry Turner had been acting as if he wasn't paying attention, but bounded from his seat mounting an objection to the question. "Your Honor, what is the relevance?"

"I will allow the question. Answer the doctor and remember you are under oath."

After a long pause for reflection about whether she was going to lie about lying, she carefully and defensively began to answer. "Situations arise in which the facts are such that we have to be very careful what we say or do not say, but no we do not lie for our clients."

Dr. Stanley wanted the jury to hear the double talk from this pundit's mouth.

"Take us through an example of a situation in which you had to be careful what you said or did not say to the public while representing an insurance company in a touchy situation."

"Your Honor, this is ridiculous!" the District Attorney screamed.

"What is your point, Doctor?" the judge inquired.

"This is the prosecution's witness. I wish to show the jury what goes on at the insurance companies and how the public relations people handle it."

"I will allow it."

Amy Nater used the break to attempt to formulate some kind of an answer. "I'm not allowed to give out specifics about a company I represent. However, we had a case that made the newspaper recently. We were accused of not paying for a treatment for one of our clients."

"By client, you mean patient, don't you?"

"We call them clients. Anyway, the company was being unfairly treated in the media, so we stepped in and improved the public's perspective on the situation."

"Did the patient get the treatment?"

"Our doctors reviewed the case and concluded that after conservative measures had failed, the treatment was allowed."

"Are you aware of a situation in which a health insurance company recommended a more expensive study or medication for a patient than was ordered?"

One of the jurors broke into a smile. Recently, his insurance company had forced him to change the blood pressure medication which had controlled his hypertension for five years to a generic alternative. The pharmacist had explained to him that it was not the generic for his drug, but one in the same class of drugs. He was angry because it was not working as well as his old drug.

"I'm not sure of the specifics on how that works. Our doctors care for our clients and would likely do this if it was warranted, but I'm not sure."

"It seems your expertise diminishes as the questions get tougher."

Henry Turner was livid. "He is harassing the witness, Your Honor!"

"Take it easy," the judge placated Henry. "Doc, ask questions only. The jury will disregard the statement made by the doctor."

"So, you say that the insurance companies do routinely recommend more expensive studies and medications?"

"I am not saying that at all."

"Well what are you saying, or as you put it, not saying about their policies?"

"I'm not sure. They have doctors who make that call."

"Have you ever heard of one case, ever, in which an insurance company called a doctor and recommended a more expensive drug or study?"

"No."

The doctor paused for effect. He looked at the jury. He sensed approval from a couple of the jurors.

"You mentioned doctors who work for insurance companies. Have you ever met any of them?"

"No, I can't say that I have."

"What are the specialties of the doctors who work for insurance companies?"

"I am told that multiple specialties are represented."

"Are these doctors in practice?"

"No, they work for the insurance company. They're hired as medical review officers."

"So, the doctors are employees of the insurance companies, and are paid by the insurance companies to review medical cases?"

"Yes, that is correct."

"Do they get bonuses related to how much money they save the insurance company?"

"Yes, as they should. Many of the..."

"Just answer the question asked of you, please," Dr. Stanley interrupted.

Amy Nater was now red faced. She was pissed off that the doctor had boxed her into this corner.

"Is it unusual for a retired kidney specialist to rule on testing for patients with heart problems?"

"I don't know how that works."

"Have you ever done PR work for an insurance company that was accused of just that? Remember, you are under oath."

"It's possible, but there have been so many unwarranted accusations in the past that..."

"Your Honor, will you make her answer the questions, please," Dr. Stanley again interrupted.

"Answer the defendant's questions. Stop doing PR work and directly answer the questions. This is not a press conference. This is my courtroom," the judge responded.

Amy sighed. "Yes, this happens and has happened. It's a problem that the insurance companies are trying to rectify."

"Do insurance companies ever misplace, throw away, or simply shred very large claims in order to delay payments?"

"Absolutely not! They do not behave that way!"

"How do you feel about a national healthcare system or single payer system for the United States?"

"I'm opposed to it. It's not necessary. We do not need socialized medicine in a democracy. It's un-American."

"What would happen to the health insurance industry if such a shift in the system were to occur?"

"It would vanish, and that is not what Americans want. Look at the Veterans Administration Healthcare System, for God's sake. Is that what you want for all of America?"

"Your Honor, she asked me a question, may I answer it?"

"No, you may not."

George continued: "Do you think healthcare is a privilege or an entitlement?"

"It's the same privilege as eating. Go to the grocery store and tell them you're hungry, but have no money. How far is that going to get you? Many people elect not to have health insurance. It is like electing not to have full coverage insurance on a vehicle, wrecking it, and then blaming others."

"Your Honor, that's all." George Stanley concluded.

The Judge pronounced: "Very well, that concludes the prosecution's case. We will adjourn, and reconvene on Monday with the defense's case. Doctor, I've sent out the subpoenas you've requested. I must say, I've not called a more interesting and diverse group to court in all my 25 years." He tapped the gavel lightly. "Court adjourned."

# CHAPTER EIGHTEEN

"What is this bullshit?" the DA protested. "How can a defendant call the prosecutor as a witness?"

"The judge surely won't allow it," the assistant DA consoled the agitated prosecutor.

"Who knows what'll happen in this circus. How much you want to bet the judge lets it slide?"

\* \* \*

"Is the defense ready to present its case?" queried Judge Armstrong.

"Yes, Your Honor. I wish to call my first witness: Henry Turner."

The courtroom erupted. The gavel slammed as though it were intended to be demolished. Finally the noise level fell below that of the screaming judge.

"I want the courtroom cleared of all non-essential people. I warned you all and you failed to heed my warning."

The bailiff did as he was asked, trying to decide what the judge meant by non-essential. He allowed family, law clerks, 'national' media reporters, and the camera crews to remain. He asked each party if they had anyone special they wanted present. All seemed happy with the contingent remaining.

Judge Armstrong beckoned both George Stanley and Henry Turner to the bench.

"Your Honor, what in the world is the defendant going to ask me?" Henry complained.

"I'm sure I don't know. Let's go to the chambers and discuss the matter," the judge responded in a hushed voice.

Away from the courtroom observers, the Judge informed George, "Well, Doc, we normally would not allow the defendant to put his prosecutor on the witness stand, nor would any defense lawyer want to do so. You'll have to come up with a very good reason for me to allow this."

"I have some 'lawyer' questions, some legal questions, that I want answered in front of the jury." Dr. Stanley outlined his questions to the dismay of Mr. Turner and the delight of the judge.

"I will allow it," chortled the Judge after only a moment of reflection.

"Your Honor, this is crazy!" Henry Turner cried.

"He has to have a defense. I'll allow him latitude in order to structure one."

Back in the courtroom, the doctor began: "Mr. Turner, how many criminal cases have your tried?"

"A little over five hundred."

"You would consider yourself an expert at criminal law?"

Henry shrugged his shoulders in an ill-disguised display of false modesty, "Yes I would."

"Tell the jury of a trial you have lost as a result of the jury ruling the crime justifiable."

"Objection!" the assistant DA yelled.

"Sustained," ordered the judge. "Rephrase the question and make it more specific."

"If you walked into the scene of a bank robbery, and the robber had a gun aimed at teller's head, would you be prosecuted if you shot the robber?"

"Likely not."

"Why not?"

Henry kicked himself for not being more vague in his response. He now saw where the doctor was going with this. "One might assume that because the teller's life was in danger, that homicide was justifiable."

"Thank you, that's all."

The Judge looked at the prosecution's table. "Do you wish to cross-examine the witness?"

The assistant DA arose: "Mr. Turner, how many criminal cases have you tried in which the defendants felt justified in their crimes?"

"One hundred percent of the five hundred cases that I have tried. Many of these people have very compelling cases for their crimes. However, if you commit a crime, the law demands that you pay for it, no matter how lofty the reason."

"No more questions, Your Honor."

"Mr. Turner, you are dismissed."

Henry rose and quickly walked the twenty-five feet back to the prosecution table, huffing with anxiety as much as with the exertion.

"Do you need a break, Mr. Turner?" asked the judge.

Not wanting to look weak in front of the jury, he declined the needed break.

"I wish to call Dr. Jerry Turen," Dr. Stanley ordered.

The witness was sworn in.

"What is your profession?" Dr. Stanley began.

"I'm a professor of medicine."

"Are you familiar with the Hippocratic oath?"

"Why, yes I am. It is the oath that new doctors take upon graduation from medical school."

"Does it address a doctor's duty to the health and welfare of his patient?"

"Yes it does. The patient's health and welfare come above and beyond any other concern."

"What if the doctor may be harmed in the process?"

"It is implied that we should all but lay down our lives for patients. The life of the patient is to be protected."

"What if someone is doing harm to a patient. Is this addressed?"

"Not directly, but it is certainly heavily implied that we are not to stand around and allow harm to be done to patients. It says, 'we first do no harm.' I interpret this to mean that we do not allow harm to be done, either. A doctor can't stand by and allow his patient to be harmed. Somebody has to fight for the patients." The frustration in the professor's voice was apparent.

"Thank you. That's all the questions I have for this witness." Good old Dr. Turen. Dr. Stanley knew he was going to be able to count on him to give a good and moral response. He had been Dr. Stanley's favorite professor in medical school, because he truly believed in the highest ideals of medicine.

"Mr. Turner," the judge summoned.

"Dr. Turen, does the Hippocratic Oath condone kidnapping?" the DA asked in cross examination.

"No."

"Does the oath condone committing criminal acts?"

"No, it does not."

"No more questions, Your Honor," Mr. Turner concluded smugly.

"The witness is dismissed," the judge proclaimed. "Next witness."

Dr. Stanley ignored the gloating of the DA as he retreated to the prosecution table. He doubted Mr. Turner would find anything to gloat over with the next witness. "I wish to call Lynn Hammond to the witness stand," he announced. Mr. Hammond trudged to the stand and cleared his throat, looking wearily in George's direction as he waited to be questioned. "What is your job title, Mr. Hammond?"

The dowdy-looking man in his drab but expensive suit looked about as excitable as a lawn chair. He answered without a trace of enthusiasm, "I'm a lobbyist for the health insurance industry." He reminded George of Donald Trump.

"Explain what it is you do, exactly."

"I lobby congress to vote for the interest of the insurance industry," Mr. Hammond explained, in a manner that made it apparent he'd spoken those very words many more times in his life than he'd cared to.

"What do you mean by lobby?" George continued, purposefully making eye contact with his jurors.

"I encourage the congressmen, by educating them on the pertinent issues relating to health insurance, to vote in a manner favorable to our industry."

"How much money does the insurance industry spend a year to encourage congress?" Dr. Stanley asked with a quick glance over at Henry Turner, who appeared to have suddenly found the ceiling tiles very interesting.

"I'm not sure."

"Would five hundred million dollars a year be a reasonable guess?"

"Yes, it would."

"What is your salary?"

"About five hundred thousand dollars per year." Mr. Hammond shifted his weight, a little self-conscious about having to reveal his personal income in front of an audience.

"How do you encourage and educate the congress?"

"We make sure that their campaigns are well funded. We have dinners for them and support their causes in any way we can."

"So you buy their support?" Dr. Stanley pressed.

Mr. Hammond, suddenly aware of how much like a bribery operation his work was coming across as, responded with an edge of indignation, "I wouldn't put it that way. We only use legal and above board means to lobby. There is competition for the votes of the congressmen. This is how it works in America."

"Would congressmen lose the support of the insurance industry if they decided to vote against the insurance companies?"

"Yes, that is likely," Mr. Hammond admitted, back to the bored monotone he'd started out with. "But those are the ones that need lobbying. We never turn our back on someone if they vote against us on occasion." He actually didn't care one way or the other, as long as he got his paycheck. He wasn't passionate about his work; he'd just sort of fallen into it. It had been so long since he had pursued an interest other than financial security, he'd forgotten whether he even had any outside interests.

"What about a congress member who is a professed opponent of the insurance industry?" George asked as he circled closer in an attempt to regain the undivided attention of his witness, who appeared to be daydreaming and on the verge of falling asleep.

"Well, in politics, you always have both friends and enemies," the lobbyist replied sleepily. "If someone's your opponent, then obviously you're not going to help them get elected."

"So, your industry donates money to the friends of the industry, thus buying their votes?"

"We donate money, but they vote how they wish." Mr. Hammond looked at his watch, wondering what his wife was cooking for dinner. He'd been a lobbyist for so many years he could have answered these questions in his sleep.

"How important is money in a campaign?" Dr. Stanley inquired, hoping he was driving the point home so that it was blatantly obvious to the jury.

"Very important, it's very expensive to run for office in this country."

"Do candidates with the most money win the elections?" the doctor urged the fatigued lobbyist.

"It certainly helps to have the funding to properly run in an election. You're not going to win without it, no matter what your message is."

"Thank you. No further questions." George was pleased with the way this testimony had gone. He looked over at the jury box. Several of the jurors were jotting down notes to themselves. That was a good sign.

"Mr. Turner, any questions?" asked the judge.

"I have no questions for this witness, Your Honor."

The judge dismissed the lobbyist. "Next?"

"I would like to call Congressman Hugh Trulock to the stand," the doctor ordered. He was getting more comfortable with the courtroom process.

The congressman more than made up for the enthusiasm Mr. Hammond had been lacking. His face was deeply grooved with 'smile lines,' as one might expect from a politician. However, though he was impeccably groomed, with not a hair or button out of place, he wore an open look of sincerity not so common in the political arena. There was something about his manner which made you want to trust him, something that bespoke of a whole-hearted conviction and passion for whatever he put his hand on.

"Congressman Trulock, are you a proponent of the health insurance industry?" the doctor asked.

"Absolutely not!" he exclaimed in a voice that was incongruous with his appearance; surprisingly low and guttural, as if he had swallowed a bucket of gravel. "I abhor the way the system runs."

"Why don't you like the health insurance industry?"

"Because they're the biggest bullies in Washington!" Mr. Trulock sputtered. "If you don't vote the way that they want you to vote, then you'll soon have an opponent sanctioned by the health insurance industry in the next election."

"Can health insurance companies be sued?"

"No, which is ridiculous. They hide behind the ERISA laws. In my opinion, attaching the legal rights of health insurance companies to the ERISA laws has been one of the biggest scams in America's history. ERISA stands for Employee Retirement Income Security Act and was enacted in 1974. By placing health insurance companies under this umbrella, they can only be sued in Federal court. This means that no lawyer will take the case because they are impossible to win. The American citizens have no legal rights when it comes to the health insurance industry."

"Do you have constituents who have problems paying for healthcare?"

"Of course I do!" the congressman fired back at the doctor impatiently. "It's the number one concern in my district. The most common request from my voters is to help them with medical issues. Usually, they're needing help getting on government programs or getting their medications. I have a staff member who does little else but try to help these folks."

"Do you get any complaints about insurance companies?" the doctor asked.

"So many that I refuse to allow them to lobby me. I refuse to talk with their lobbyists. I have an obligation to represent my people. In fact, I see so much suffering that I'm 100% in support of a national healthcare system; one in which all patients will receive free care and medications." George listened intently, silently cheering his congressman on. He looked around to make sure the news cameras were rolling. He couldn't have asked for a better witness if he had put the words in this gentleman's mouth himself.

"Who is going to pay for this?" George now turned again to ask the fired-up politician.

"I look at the salaries of the CEOs of the insurance companies, the salaries of some of the doctors, the 'cottage industry' that has arisen in the plaintiff malpractice community, and the legions of bureaucracy in our current system, and I see plenty of money. This money is all being wasted. If we did away with our current system, we could provide care and medication for those who need it. There would be plenty of money available."

"What about those who want the current system?"

"If a man who has no insurance and takes home $25,000 per year gets ill, as much as I love America and hate to say this, he is better off in Canada or Europe. He may have a medical bill which exceeds his salary by $250,000, ten times what he makes. Most, when saddled with this happenstance, just have to walk away or file bankruptcy. If they attempt to pay the bill and can't meet the payments, they may lose their home. Our citizens would be better off if the bill was less and paid by the government. This would keep costs down. Right now, the hospitals punish those who pay for those who don't, in order to make enough to stay open. For those who like the current system, it could stay intact, to some degree as it is today, as a fee for service option. You would simply elect which system you wanted to use."

George nodded appreciatively to Mr. Trulock and turned to the judge. "That's all I have for the congressman, Your Honor."

"Mr. Turner, do you have any questions?" Judge Armstrong asked doubtfully.

"No, Your Honor, I enjoyed hearing the congressman's platform, but I'm not sure what he's doing here. This is a court of law, not a political rally!"

Judge Armstrong leaned forward and spoke down his nose at the DA, "It is for me to determine what's appropriate for this courtroom, understood? I will allow the doctor to defend himself how he wishes, even if it is non-traditional."

Without missing a beat, George announced: "My final witness, Your Honor, is Robert Wesley."

"Oh yes," the judge scrolled down his notes. "Mr. Wesley does not want to be here with us today, but I have forced him to. He feels it unfair that he has to testify, so he is labeled a hostile witness," Judge Armstrong explained to the jury.

"What is your occupation?" Dr. Stanley asked. As he'd suspected, Mr. Wesley avoided looking him in the eye. He hoped the sworn courtroom oath would be enough to ensure his cooperation.

"I am the Vice President for Operations at Cherokee Hills Hospital."

"How do we know one another?" George asked innocently.

"I was the head of the management company which ran your office when you were in practice in our area."

"Did you ever work at D.J.S. insurance company?"

"Yes, I did."

"What was your job title?"

"I was the Director of Financial Operations."

Switching gears, Dr. Stanley urged Mr. Wesley to "explain to the jury what an insurance claim is."

"It's what is sent to the insurance company in order for the client to receive payment. It's a bill to the insurance company."

"Did you ever have occasion to shred claims that happened to be a great expense to the insurance company? Remember, you are under oath."

Doctor Stanley had come up close to the witness as he continued the interrogation. One night when they had gone out for beers, Robert Wesley had confidentially told George about some of the unbelievable practices of his former company. He never expected his old friend to make him admit to it in public. He caught the doctor's eye and mouthed, "Fuck you!"

"Did the witness have a response? I thought I saw your mouth move," the doctor said, flashing his old buddy an apologetic grin.

"I did, and I'm embarrassed to say it, shred large claims while I worked for D.J.S That was a long time ago, and I'm sure this is not a common practice." He hoped none of the higher ups at Delsay would get wind of his confession. Though he'd actually quit because he was disgusted with Delsay's moral conduct, or rather lack of it, he still received monthly payments from the company as part of a tidy little severance package.

"Yes, the insurance industry has certainly cleaned up its act, hasn't it?" George agreed facetiously.

"Objection, Your Honor. The defendant is testifying," Henry barked.

"Sustained. Just ask the questions, and make no commentary."

Dr. Stanley looked into the jury box, and knew he'd made an impact. The jury was a seething cauldron of anger. George knew that each and every juror had likely had some negative experience with insurance. He circled back around to again face his witness. "Can you prove that they have changed their policy of shredding expensive claims?"

"No, I'm no longer employed by the insurance company," Mr. Wesley sighed.

Dr. Stanley sat back down. "That's all, Your Honor."

"Mr. Turner, any questions for the witness?"

"No, Your Honor, let's just get this ridiculous case over with."

"Very well, then. We'll adjourn today, returning tomorrow for closing remarks," the judge announced. Judge Rudy Armstrong deemed himself a "Pillar of Justice." He prided himself on his ability to lend an impartial eye to any case, no matter how heart-wrenching. As the session closed, he was deeply troubled to realize he'd lost his distance... he was siding with the defendant. He didn't personally know anyone who had experienced a scandalous insurance situation, but his sense of justice and equality for all was so deeply engrained that the thought of any of these companies *shredding* large claims rattled him to the core. A debilitating disease or accident could strike anyone, even his brother or daughters and their families, even himself. And now to learn that no law-abiding premium-paying citizen could have any trust in their health insurance, it made his head reel.

The judge forgot to strike the gavel before leaving the bench. He had become disoriented as his mind reeled with anger. *How do they sleep at night! Shredding documents and denying claims.* He had to gain control of himself. It was only the surprised murmurs and whisperings of those in the courtroom wondering whether they were truly dismissed that clued him into what he'd just forgotten to do. He almost turned around and went back to strike that gavel, but then decided against it and eased his way out of the courtroom. He'd built up too much of a reputation as judge to admit the mistake and have people think he was getting senile.

# CHAPTER NINETEEN

"You're up, Mr. Turner," Judge Armstrong called, in a tone that ordered silence in the buzzing courtroom.

Henry wore his darkest blue suit, hoping to convey to the jurors that he meant business. He took his time walking to the jury box, standing quietly for a moment of reflection.

"The reason we have trials in America is to allow everyone, no matter how stark naked guilty that they are, a chance at justice. Dr. George Stanley has paraded a bizarre sundry of inconsequential witnesses before you in order to confuse the issue. I intentionally did not object at every opportunity. I did not cross-examine any witness who was of no value to this case, so we could quickly get to the point we are at today. That point is the point of justice. Three men were kidnapped and tortured. We have seen video evidence of this. It is damning, incontrovertible, and the defendant provided us with the DVD. We have a surrender and a confession."

Henry Turner walked away from the jurors in dramatic form and pointed in the face of the doctor.

"He must be found guilty. No matter how much you hate your insurance company, you can't use this as a reason to set this man loose. He is unstable and dangerous to society. There is no Robin Hood!" Henry walked back to his table and took a seat.

Dr. Stanley had worn a suit for the first time without any medical appendage…And for the first time in the trial, he was a little nervous. He took a deep breath and rose to face the jurors.

"I come before you today and ask that you reach inside yourselves. I want you to reach down and try to locate the compassion that God has given us all…the compassion for our brothers and sisters…the compassion for other living and breathing human beings. Deep down in every human heart is a sense of justice. A moral compass we sometimes call a conscious. I want you to use it today. If you help your neighbor by doing something illegal, is that wrong? If you don't help them by doing something legal is that right? You have to answer these questions in your hearts."

George walked to his table and took a sip of water, readying himself. He hoped this would work. He looked out at the rows of spectators and found Susan, watching from the aisle seat of the second row. Her eyes met his, consoling him, encouraging him on. *Okay, here goes nothing*, he thought, scanning the expectant faces of his jury.

"I want you to close your eyes, go ahead and close them, and envision your child drowning in a river. You are at the edge of the bank of the river and you reach out your hand to your drowning child. Your fingertips touch and you try to clasp your hands around theirs. All of a sudden you are pulled off the bank and thrown to the ground. You watch helplessly as your baby is sucked under the strong current. You scream, but to no avail. You look up to see who has caused your child to die, and it is the CEO of your insurance company. He has a wad of money in his hand and thanks you for your business as he walks away. This has been my nightmare. Open your eyes."

Several of the female, and one of the male jurors had tears in their eyes.

"I could not stand around and watch patients and family drown in pain and in the horrors of their illness, while the insurance companies profited. My nightmare worsened as I saw more and more injustice. I was consumed with anger and had to act to save patients' lives. You heard Henry say that if I had shot a bank robber, I would be a free man. You heard my professor say that I had a duty to protect the lives of my patients at any cost. You heard how the insurance companies have fought legislation that may help the patients. You can't even sue them for God's sake! They own congress, by their own admission. Finally, you have heard, by a first hand account of a reluctant witness, how these companies behave; shredding large claims in order to prevent paying a large bill. The only thing that they care about is making money. I could care less how much they make if they would put the patients well being first. However, as you have seen, that is not what these companies do."

George paused and swallowed, trying to ignore the lump in his throat which always choked him up when he thought of his wife.

"I don't have the nightmare any longer. In my nightmare, it was my wife slipping away from me, not a child. You all recall what I told you about my wife?"

Several of the jurors nodded their heads, indicating yes.

"I lacked the knowledge or the courage to save my wife. I simply believed what I was told and let her die. I want you, the jury, to send a message to all Americans. I want you to tell them that enough is enough. Something has got to give. To set your minds at ease, Robin Hood will retire to a more peaceful protest. As a free man I will continue to dedicate my life to lobbying for patients in this country."

"I beg of you to save the children from drowning. Allow doctors to help their patients. Don't let the insurance companies pull them away from the healing shores in order to save money. Doctors and patients live in this nightmare every day. You can help stop it."

With that, Dr. Stanley sat down. There, he thought, I did it. He thought he would feel relief once he got to the end of his closing statement, and he did feel some relief. But he felt drained.

The judge gave his final instructions to the jury, and the bailiffs ushered all of the spectators out of the courtroom, allowing George only a moment of contact with Susan. "You look pale," she told him, fretting over whether they were feeding him enough in prison. Never had she felt so much like a worried mother. George appreciated her concern, but didn't say much. He felt distant, disconnected. "Get some sleep tonight," she ordered. He nodded compliantly, but he knew he wouldn't sleep. The court emptied. Everyone but George went home.

On every trial date, the half-hour trip from prison to the courthouse and back was the highlight of the day for George. The sky was always there to accompany his ride away from and back to the constant unearthly fluorescent light of his jail cell. He imagined dissolving himself into the wind and slipping away into the atmosphere with the birds and insects, the clouds and the sun, where everything was open, unending, free.

Actually, the inside of the prison was not all that different from the inside of the hospital…the same disconnect from the outside natural world, the same endless maze of halls and cells (though in the hospital they were called rooms), the same sterile smells of cleaning solutions used by janitors on the floors and walls, the same institutional food. The only difference was that he was like the prison wardens when he was at the hospital…he got to go home every day…now, confined in a prison cell, he was like a patient awaiting recovery, hoping for the day he'd get to walk out the doors into the daylight again. He never had realized how much he took the sun and its daily orb around the planet for granted. He knew he was likely prison bound, but as he leaned his forehead against the window of the armored van, and felt all the cells and pores in his upturned face soaking up the warmth of the late afternoon sun, he couldn't help feeling a glimmer of hope that this was his last van ride for a while.

\*   \*   \*

"Has the jury reached a verdict?" asked the judge.

"We have, Your Honor," the foreman spoke.

The bailiff handed the verdict over to Judge Armstrong. George watched as the judge gingerly opened the sheet of paper, read it, and presented it back to the officer. Though the doctor had expertise in reading people, the judge had expertise in not being read. George, along with everyone in the courtroom and beyond, awaited the verdict in suspense.

"All rise while the jury reads the verdict," commanded the judge.

"On the three counts of kidnapping, we the jury, find the doctor not guilty."

George Stanley remained poised for a moment, then lowered his face to his hands.

The judge ignored the swell of response from the crowd. "The defendant is free to go and the case is dismissed."

Only when retreated to the privacy of his chambers did the honorable Judge Rudy Armstrong lift his head to the Heavens, heave an immense sigh of relief, and whisper, "Thank you, dear God; there is some justice on this miserable planet!"

Dr. Susan Harrison, who had been watching with dread from the front row and nervously chewing her nails until her cuticles bled, rushed to George's side and embraced him. He was shaking like a leaf. He couldn't believe it was over; everything he'd been planning for and fighting for coming to one single simple verdict…'not guilty.' He was numb with relief.

Reporters raced out the doors with their cell phones to their ears. Henry Turner did not move from the prosecution table. He glared unprofessionally at the jury. The buzzing of the media outside the courtroom became a dull roar as they learned the news. 'Robin Hood is free!' was the victory cry heard among the protestors. The unrequited love triangles and murderous threats of the daily soaps on TV were interrupted by the breaking story. A podium was set up outside of the courtroom for a press conference featuring the newly freed doctor. Only when the media had followed the doctor and his entourage out of the courtroom, did the prosecution sneak away from the hubbub and retreat through a side door, hoping to avoid the humiliation of being hammered with the prying questions of the reporters. And only once Dr. George Stanley set foot outside the courthouse doors without his handcuffs did he truly taste what it felt to be free.

"Here they come!" shouted one of the reporters on the courtroom steps.

George gripped Susan's hand like he was never going to let go as he approached the podium. Susan searched his face, wondering how he must be feeling after the whole ordeal he'd just been through. She didn't need to ask; it was apparent in the light that danced in his eyes. She had never seen him so buoyant, so unencumbered. It was like he'd been shackled with heavy weights all the time she'd known him and now he'd stepped out of the shackles. It was only now that he beamed with clarity and moved with a spring in step that she realized how much weight he had carried with him. Even before she discovered his Robin Hood identity, even when they had joked and dated and made love, there had been a dark shadow about him that she'd failed to acknowledge at the time. Now, as he turned his benevolent gaze on her, she began to wonder for the first time if happy endings really were possible.

"How do you feel?" shouted a CNN reporter.

"I'm overwhelmed," he laughed. "I have a renewed faith in the American people. I asked for the jury to send a message to the insurance industry and to the politicians. The message is that it is time for a change. They were thinking outside of the box, so to speak, in the jury room. They did the right thing."

"Samantha Huet, AJC, what kind of change do we need?"

"One of several things has to happen. We need to have radical changes in the monitoring of the health insurance industry. They need to be treated like a utility company, in which they can only make so much profit in a year. That way, they are not totally profit driven. Another solution would be a tiered healthcare system. A National Healthcare System for those who opted for it, and a private system for those who wanted it and could afford it. A final option would be a Canadian type system, in which healthcare and medications are free to all."

"Which would you prefer?" Samantha asked, dodging the elbow of the NBC reporter trying to push in beside her. She was pleased that 'her' story was ending on a positive note. Even though a win for the insurance company would have meant more drama, the lack of drama was more than made up for in the satisfaction of a feel-good outcome. People liked happy endings. Sam counted her lucky stars that public interest hadn't died down before the trial ended, which always happened when court cases dragged on infinitely. She daydreamed about the big fat raise she was sure was waiting for her back at the office, but snapped back to reality as Dr. Stanley responded.

"I only want to see the patients treated fairly. As it is now, he-who-has-the-money makes the rules. This has to change. We can make the system we have, already in place, work for us. Whether you're a democrat or republican, a liberal or conservative, you have to concede that something's got to be done about this crazy system. If we can take the power away from the insurance companies, we can go a long way in bringing some balance to the system. Now I'm going to bring a little balance to this system," he grinned, looking at Susan.

Susan took the microphone from him and added, "And I'm going to make sure of that!" kissing her man passionately for all to see and closing her eyes to the blinding flood of light from all the flash cameras eager to get a juicy shot of the defendant in the embrace of such a sexpot.

The two doctors turned from the podium, ignoring the artillery of questions flying after them. Dr. Stanley suddenly remembered one last thing and turned back to the media, holding up a hand to halt the interrogation onslaught.

"I want to give a website address where patients can send complaints about insurance companies. We will forward these on to congress and the insurance commission. The address is www.AmericansHeldHostage.com.

George and Susan pushed their way through the crowd but stopped as they encountered Natasha, Timothy, and Debra. Natasha and George stared at one another for a moment and then George nodded his head at Timothy. Debra was the one brave enough to break the silence and gave George a huge hug.

"I love you, and what you stand for. I, well, the three of us," Debra glanced at Natasha and Timothy, "owe our lives to you."

Timothy chimed in: "Ya, man thanks. I am in school now and the doctor said that I could try out for the football team."

"That is awesome. I wish you the best," George shyly replied.

"What is you future, Doc?" inquired Natasha.

"Well, I am out of the kidnapping business, and my medical license is suspended, so I may take up fishing." Everyone laughed, but Natasha looked impatient.

"So, what's next? I mean we can't just stop here, can we?" she asked.

"Remember what Robin Hood stands for," Dr. Stanley began. "I took away the freedom of three CEOs so that the three of you could regain yours. But, with that freedom comes responsibility. It is your job to fight for the freedom of all patients in this country. Do not rest a day until you see a change. You are public figures now and everyone will be watching you. Are you going to waste this gift of life or are you going to use it? Show others how to fight for their freedom. We have their attention now! It is your time to shine."

Natasha was crying as George and Susan started to walk toward Susan's car. In a quick rush, she pulled George back and threw her arms around him. "Thank you, Robin Hood."

"You're welcome." It was all that George needed.

As George and Susan drove away from the courthouse, George started to smile. "Um, back at the jail, you said that you wanted…"

Susan interrupted him quickly, "a Congressional hearing, yes."

"To have my baby," George finished his sentence, undeterred.

"If Robin Hood is up to some merriment, I do."

The two laughed and held hands as they drove away.

— THE END —

# ACKNOWLEDGEMENTS

We would like to thank everyone who has contributed to this novel.

Zoe Haugo made critical additions to the novel and is a talented editor.

Thanks to Dr. Ross for the healthy suggestions which added greatly to the novel.

J.K.S. wishes to remain anonymous.

# ABOUT THE AUTHOR

Neil Shulman is best known as the author and producer of the Hollywood sensation, Doc Hollywood. He has authored multiple Fiction and Non-Fiction novels.

## Fiction

The Backyard Tribe, St. Martin's Press, (hard cover), 1994
The Corporate Kid, Whitman Publishing, 2011
Finally...I'm a Doctor, Rx Humor, 1976 (hard cover), 1993 (soft cover)
The Germ Patrol: All About Shots for Tots... and Big Kids, Too!, Rx
    Humor (soft cover); co-authored with Todd Stolp, M.D. and Robin
    Voss, 1998

Life Before Sex, pre-pub edition, Rx Humor (soft cover) 1998, reprinted as The Puberty Prevention Club, Rx Humor (soft cover) 2007, DIP Publishing (soft cover) 2012

101 Ways to Know if You're a Nurse, Rx Humor (soft cover) 1998

Second Wind, Rx Humor (soft cover) 1995

What Dead...Again? Legacy (hard cover) 1979 (basis for the movie: Doc Hollywood)

What's in a Doctor's Bag? Co-authored with Sibley Fleming and Todd Stolp, M.D., Rx Humor (soft cover) 1994

Under the Backyard Sky, Co-authored with Sibley Fleming and Stan Mullins, Peachtree Publishers (hard cover) 1995

How to Have a Habit Co-authored with Todd Stolp and Robin Voss, Rx Humor (soft cover) 2002

101 Ways to Know if You're a CNA, Rx Humor (soft cover) 2002

Don't Be Afraid of the Dentist, Rx Humor (poster book) 2002

101 Ways to Know if You're a Medical Records Specialist, Rx Humor (poster book) 2003

Drive Safe, Stop Safe, (featuring Michael Jordan) Rx Humor (poster book) 2003

Spotless, Rx Humor (soft cover) 2004

The Nurse Curse, Great Quotations (calendar book) 2004

Your Body Doesn't Have Spare Parts, Great Quotations (calendar book) 2004

101 Ways to Know If You're a Medical Services Professional, Rx Humor (poster book) 2004

101 Ways to Know if You're in Retail Real Estate, Rx Humor (poster book) 2004

## Non-Fiction

The Real Truth About Aging, Co-authored with Adam Golden MD and Michael Silverman MD, Prometheus, 2009 (pending)

The Black Man's Guide to Good Health, Co-Authored with Dr. James Reed and Charlene Shucker, Perigree (soft cover) 1994, Revised Edition, Hilton Publishing, 2010 (pending)

Your Body's Red Light Warning Signals, Co-authored with Jack Birge, M.D. and Joon Ahn, M.D., Dell Publishing (soft cover)1999, Revised Edition, Bantam Dell (trade and mass paperback), 2009

Get Between the Covers: Leaving a Legacy by Writing a Book, Co-Authored with Eric Spencer, AuthorHouse, trade (soft cover) 2006

Better Health Care for Less, Co-Authored with Letitia Sweitzer, Hippocrene, trade (soft cover) 1994

High Blood Pressure, Co-authored with Dr. Elijah Saunders and Dr. W. Dallas Hall, Dell (soft cover) 1987, reprinted in 1993

Let's Play Doctor, Co-authored with Dr. Edmond Moses and Dr. Daniel Adame, Harcourt and Brace (soft cover) 1995, Rx Humor 1999

Understanding Growth Hormone, Co-authored with Letitia Sweitzer, Hippocrene (hard cover) 1993

Your Body, Your Health, Co-authored with Rowena Sobezyk, Prometheus (soft cover) 2002

Healthy Transitions. A Women's Guide to Pre-menopause. Menopause and Beyond, Prometheus (soft cover) 2004